Brother Frank's Gospel Hour

ALSO BY W. P. KINSELLA

Dance Me Outside
Scars
Shoeless Joe Jackson Comes to Iowa
Born Indian
The Moccasin Telegraph
The Thrill of the Grass
Shoeless Joe
The Iowa Baseball Confederacy
The Alligator Report
The Fencepost Chronicles
Red Wolf, Red Wolf
The Rainbow Warehouse
The Miss Hobbema Pageant
Two Spirits Soar
Box Socials
The Dixon Cornbelt League
Go the Distance
The Winter Helen Dropped By
If Wishes Were Horses

Brother Frank's Gospel Hour

STORIES BY
W·P·KINSELLA

SOUTHERN METHODIST UNIVERSITY PRESS

Dallas

Copyright © 1994 by W. P. Kinsella
First Southern Methodist University Press edition, 1996
Published by arrangement with HarperCollins Publishers Ltd., Toronto
All rights reserved

Requests for permission to reproduce material from
this work should be sent to:
    Rights and Permissions
    Southern Methodist University Press
    PO Box 750415
    Dallas, Texas 75275-0415

"The Elevator" first appeared in *Canadian Fiction Magazine* in a
slightly different form.

LIBRARY OF CONGRESS CATALOGING-IN-PUBLICATION DATA
Kinsella, W. P.
    Brother Frank's gospel hour : stories / by W.P. Kinsella. —
1st Southern Methodist University Press ed.
        p.   cm.
    ISBN 0-87074-398-8 (cloth : acid-free paper). —
ISBN 0-87074-399-6 (paper : acid-free paper)
    I. Title.
PR9199.3.K443B76   1996
813'.54—dc20   96-34545

Cover photograph of W. P. Kinsella by Barbara Turner
Cover design by Tom Dawson Graphic Design

Printed in the United States of America on acid-free paper
10 9 8 7 6 5 4 3 2 1

*For my grandsons
Jason Kirk Kinsella
Kurtis William Kinsella
and
Max Knight Kinsella*

Contents

Brother Frank's Gospel Hour

Bull

It ain't very often that my friend Frank Fencepost gets real mail. He sometimes refer to himself as the King of Junkmail though, because he put himself on every trash mailing list in North America, get bulletins and advertisements from every church, cuckoo-clock maker, stamp dealer, and political party there is. But only about twice a year do anything arrive in a *white* envelope, one that don't have either a plastic window in it or Frank's name typed on by a computer.

This white envelope is covered with about three dollars' worth of stamps, have the word *Registered* in big red letters in two or three places. In order to claim it Frank have to sign his name in a book that Ben Stonebreaker keep behind the counter at the general store.

"First time I got a registered letter wasn't from a collection agency," say Frank, hold it up to the sunshine, try to guess what's in it.

The last time Frank got a registered letter from a collection agency, he read it real quick, smile big, crumple up the letter what got red writing all over it and the word URGENT in inch-high capitals, throw it away. He heave a big sigh and say, "Sure happy that outfit ain't gonna bother me no more. They say this here is their final notice."

Today's envelope is thick and have the Alberta Provincial Seal on the outside.

"You can open it," we say. "It addressed to you. It not like you sneaking a look at somebody else's mail."

"Right!" says Frank, look a little sheepish. "I knew that."

"Hey, I got to go to court," Frank yell. "First time I get to be the witness instead of the criminal."

"Why do you have to go to court?" we all want to know.

Turn out the place Frank have to go to is the Alberta Supreme Court, while the reason is on account of he got fired from a job last summer. It was a job he never should of had.

Frank is really good at getting himself hired on at jobs he ain't qualified for.

"I create qualifications," Frank argue. "Qualifications are a state of mind. Besides, I don't see the newspaper full of ads for what I do best. I keep looking for ads that say 'Handsome Indian Wanted,' or 'Great Lover Wanted,' but all I see are jobs for burger flippers and telephone solicitors. You know the kind, 'Make $100,000 a week in your spare time.'"

Like me, Frank been studying at the Tech School in Wetaski-win for the last few years on how to repair tractors. But there never seem to be any jobs in that line.

On the other hand, women, whether they is old or young, white or Indian, is usually charmed by Frank. But what really surprises me is that he can con men almost as easy as women. I was there the day he got hired for that job he shouldn't have had — foreman for Mr. Manley Carstairs at the C Bar C Ranch.

The day before, Frank seen the ad in the *Wetaskiwin Times* advertise for a ranch foreman.

"Let's drive out there," Frank say. "The job's as good as mine."

"You never even lived on a farm," I say.

"Hey, a foreman tells other people what to do. I can do that. 'Haul that hay! Fix that fence! Spread that manure! Brand those cattle! Get me a beer!' Silas, to get any job, all I got to do is look the part, act confident, and lie like a snake."

We drive out to the C Bar C Ranch, which south of Camrose. It must be worth a million dollars; the house is a mansion, and there are two Cadillacs and a Lincoln parked in the driveway.

Mr. Manley Carstairs is about fifty, short with a big belly; wear a white cowboy hat, a sky-blue western suit, and $500 boots. The three of us walk around the farmyard while Mr. Carstairs explain the job.

Inside of two minutes, Frank walking with the same gait as Mr. Carstairs, got a timothy straw at the same angle in his mouth. In another two minutes Frank even talk a little like Mr. Carstairs. And even though Frank don't have much of a belly he walk with it pushed out in front of him the same way as the boss of the C Bar C.

"Just call me Foreman Frank," he say, make a polite little laugh, and reel off the names of several ranches where he claim to have worked. He got the ranch names from a clerk at the Wetaskiwin Seed and Feed Store.

"I guess I'm what you'd call a progressive Indian," Frank say. "I work for you as foreman, but I'm sure you won't mind that three nights a week I go to Edmonton, study at the University of Alberta to get my degree in social work. My ultimate goal is to help my people."

Mr. Manley Carstairs eat this up just like Frank feeding him candy.

"Which," Frank go on, "is the reason I brought this unfortunate fellow here." And Frank point at me. "This young man is one of those Indians who live off government handouts, never done an honest day's work in his life. But I aim to change all that. With a menial position for him here on the ranch, and what with me supervising, why I'll see that he works. You know how most of these Indians are if you don't watch them all the time."

Frank is talking Mr. Manley Carstairs' language. They are buddies now. Mr. Carstairs forget all about references and experience. He can't hire Frank fast enough.

"My friend's Indian name is Standing-neck-deep-in-slough-water, but we just call him Stan. You won't give him no job where he has to read or write, or anything that might embarrass him. He has some pride, even if he don't look like it. First pay check I'll see that he buys some decent clothes. He don't have any idea how to handle money either, so it'll be okay for you to give me his pay for safekeeping. I'll see that it don't all get spent in one place." Frank kind of leer at Mr. Carstairs when he say that.

"Does he speak English?" Mr. Carstairs ask.

"Only enough to be dangerous. Ain't that right, Stan?"

"Right, Foreman Frank," I say, raise my hand up in front of me the way Indians do on television.

"Say, does your range go on for a long ways?" Frank ask.

"Over six hundred thousand acres. I guess you could say that's a good ways. Why do you ask?"

"It's just that my specialty is long-range planning," say Frank.

Mr. Carstairs slap Frank on the back and laugh and laugh.

"What do you figure to do, now you've got the job?" I ask Frank on the drive home.

"I figure I'll just ask the cowboys what needs to be done, and then I'll tell them to do it."

There was another registered letter arrive at Hobbema General Store, addressed to Standing-neck-deep-in-slough-water, but that letter never get claimed.

Both Frank and me are a little surprised to find there aren't any criminals in this trial. It's what is called a civil case: Carstairs vs. Ace Artificial Insemination Inc. I have to look up *civil* in the dictionary. There are about a dozen definitions, but some of the words mean the same as civil are *polite, courteous,* and *gallant.* It take a long time to figure out what is going on, but after a day or so, I understand that Mr. Carstairs, who raise purebred Charolais cattle, so white they look like snowbanks scattered about the fields, is mad. The Ace Artificial Insemination Inc. made his purebred cows pregnant, but what come out wasn't purebred Charolais calves, but plug-ugly little mavericks.

Mr. Carstairs want his money back from AAII, plus a lot of damages for the purebred calves he didn't get. The AAII say they did everything right. The cows must have already been pregnant. Mr. Carstairs say there was no way the cows could have been pregnant.

"What going on here is like fighting in slow motion," I say to Frank.

"How so?"

"Well, it's a little like walking up to a guy in a bar, one who's been staring you down all evening, and saying friendly, as if you talking to a school teacher, 'Excuse me, motherfucker, but you've been giving me the evil eye, and if you don't stop I'm gonna kick the piss out of you.'

"Then the other guy says, polite as you please, 'Fuck off, asshole. I wasn't looking at you.' Even when the fight start, it done in slow motion. Maybe that dude punch me in the face, knock me over a couple of tables, then I get up and kick him in the crotch. He pull a razor out of his boot and come for me. I take a gun from inside my jacket, we stare at each other and circle, all the time calling each other names, but polite as you please. Then the RCMP come along tell us both to behave or they'll do us a certain amount of damage.

"The fighters is like the lawyers, and the RCMP is like the judge."

The lawyers talk lawyer talk, but I'm able to translate enough to explain it mainly about how Ace Artificial Insemination Inc. collect samples of bull semen, and how they got foolproof ways to see the samples stay pure until they reach the cow.

Frank get all excited.

"I can do that," he says. "I'll collect my own samples, then I'll stop pretty ladies on the street and say, 'Pardon me, Ma'am, but for only $500 you can have a baby look just like me. I'll make a million dollars in no time."

"I'm not sure the world is ready for that idea," I say.

When it is Frank's turn to testify, the bailiff try to swear him in.

"Do you swear to tell the truth, the whole truth, and nothing but the truth?"

"I'll take the first one," say Frank.

Even the judge have to smile at that.

"'I do' will suffice," say the bailiff.

"Why would you give me a choice if I got to choose all three?" ask Frank.

"The appropriate reply is 'I do,'" the bailiff say.

"If I say 'I do,' I'm liable to wind up married to somebody. How about 'Okay'?"

"Whatever."

"Let me hear those choices again?"

The bailiff look cross, but place Frank's hand on the Bible and mumble, "Do you swear to tell the truth, the whole truth, and nothing but the truth? So help you God."

"Hey, I don't believe in none of this stuff," Frank say, pushing the Bible to one side. "But I take an Indian oath to tell the truth."

The bailiff and Frank look up at the judge.

"I believe that will be in order," he say, and sigh.

Frank, he leap down off the witness chair. He wearing Eathen Firstrider's beaded buckskin jacket, moccasins, a ten-gallon black hat on top of his braids, which his girl, Connie Bigcharles, tie for him with bright red ribbon. He shuffle along for a few feet then he crouch over, slap his palms on his legs just above the knees, and start to chant "Hoo-hoo, Hoo-hoo, Hoo-hoo," just like a train trying to pick up speed. He dance like that all around the lawyers' tables, stop to stare down the blouse of the woman who taking everything down on a tiny typewriter. Then he work his way back to the witness stand and sit down again.

He wipe his brow. "This here witnessing is hard work," he say. "I made my peace with the Great Spirit. I burst into flame before your very eyes if I was to tell a lie."

"His great spirits come from the Alberta Government Liquor Store," Mad Etta, our medicine lady, whisper to me.

Last night, me, Frank, Mad Etta, and a few friends closed up the Travelodge bar in Wetaskiwin. Frank got in a certain amount of trouble in the parking lot, and the skin under his eye is the red-black color of a ripe apple.

"Now, Mr. Fencepost," say the lawyer for Ace Artificial Insemination Inc., "you are employed as a foreman at the C Bar C Ranch?"

"Just call me Foreman Frank. And I used to be employed by the C Bar C. I'm practicing my unemployment right now."

"How long were you employed by the C Bar C?"

"Two or three months."

"I see." The lawyer take a deep breath.

"Could we assume, Mr. Fencepost, that, as the information before me indicates, you were employed by the C Bar C Ranch from May to July of the year in question?"

"I guess so," says Frank. "Is the *year in question* like the station to which you are listening?"

"Now, Mr. Fencepost, could you tell us the exact day you were fired?"

"The day Mr. Carstairs got mad at me."

"Could you be more specific?"

"Well, see, Mr. Carstairs and his missus was supposed to have gone into Red Deer for the day. So soon as their car pulled onto the highway why I headed up to the house. See, the Carstairs got this pretty daughter name of Virginia Jean . . ."

"You misunderstand, Mr. Fencepost, I meant more specific about the date."

"It wasn't a date. We just got together whenever her folks went out."

"*The date of the month.*"

"Virginia Jean was okay, but I'd never name her *date of the month.*"

"Mr. Fencepost, you're being very exasperating."

"Thank you. I always try to co-operate."

At this point the lawyer reserve the right to recall Frank sometime later. Guess he figure to get along better with Mr. Carstairs as a witness.

"Can you tell us," he say to Mr. Carstairs, who look like a bulldog in a dark-pink western suit and string tie, "the circumstances that led you to discharge your ranch foreman, Mr. Fencepost?"

"I can't see that that has anything to do with those swindlers," and he point a short stubby arm at the man from Ace Artificial Insemination Inc., "impregnating my purebred stock with bad quality . . ."

"Answer the question, please," say the judge.

"I caught the sneaky son of a bitch in bed with my daughter. I walked into her bedroom, and there they were. He wasn't wearing anything except his hat. He looked at me cool as you please, and he said, 'Well, Boss, are you gonna believe Foreman Frank, or are you gonna believe what you see?' Lucky for him my hand gun was in the study and my rifle was in the pick-up truck. Last I seen of him until today, was him running north, pulling on his pants and carrying his boots."

"I see. Now, was this before or after Ace Artificial Insemination Inc. made their visit to your ranch?"

Mr. Carstairs take a notebook out of his inside pocket, study the calendar part.

"It was two days before."

About an hour before, during an intermission in the trial, something happen that I was afraid was going to. Mr. Carstairs stare at me as we pass each other in the hall, then say to his lawyer, "That's the other Indian we tried to subpoena. That's Stan Standing-neck-deep-in-slough-water."

"I'm afraid you're mistaken," I say, real calm. "My name is Silas Ermineskin, and I write books. I don't associate with common riffraff like Frank Fencepost. Apparently, to you white men, all us Indians look alike."

Mr. Carstairs stare at me for quite a while, then decide that I'm telling the truth. "Stan couldn't read or write," he say to the lawyer.

After all this time he still believe some of the lies Frank told him.

At another intermission in the trial, Frank smile friendly at that lawyer for AAII.

"I bet this case really gonna do a lot for your career, eh? When you talk about the big cases you've handled you can say you was defence lawyer for some bull cum. Must make all them years of law school worthwhile."

"I see you have a sense of humor, if a somewhat primitive one," say the lawyer. "We'll talk again tomorrow, in court, Mr. Fencepost, and you may just find out what it feels like to have your hide nailed to a wall."

But before he get to Frank he take another shot at Mr. Carstairs.

"Mr. Carstairs, is it true that on your ranch there are several animals that could have impregnated your purebred cows?"

"I run a large spread and I have two other bulls, one a Hereford, and one a mixed breed. But there is no way either bull could have had access to the Charolais cows."

Then he go on to explain how the purebred cows kept in a special corral separate from all the other animals, and how they have their temperatures taken every day so the people from AAII don't arrive at a time when the cows ain't fertile.

"That's all very interesting. Still, the possibility exists, does it not, that some other animal on your farm impregnated your cows?"

Mr. Carstairs glower at the lawyer, but he grunt that the possibility exist.

"And, do you not have on your ranch a male buffalo?"

Mr. Carstairs laugh loud. Kind of an inbreathing noise like a pig might make. "That old rat's nest? My eldest daughter rescued it from a zoo when she was a little girl. People didn't want to stare at a mangy buffalo, so they were going to have it put down. It's been standing like a willow clump in the south pasture for close to fifteen years," and he laugh like a pig again.

"Irrespective of its background, this is an unemasculated male buffalo which makes its home on your ranch?"

"It is."

On the second afternoon Mr. Angstrom, the lawyer who is defending the bull semen, with the help of a lady scientist in a white smock, put on a demonstration for the court. It seem to me it must be hard for them to keep a straight face while he doing it, because one of the things they have to show the court is a plastic cow's vagina. Truth is it don't seem hard at all for Mr. Angstrom and the lady to keep their faces straight. The lady especially have a face I'd guess been straight all her life. She have the plastic model as well as charts and pictures and tubes and wires.

Mr. Angstrom hand all these things to her one at a time while she demonstrate how the bull semen is deposited in the precise spot it meant to go, and how there could never be a mix-up of any kind.

I bet people can hear Frank chuckling and slapping his thigh all the way out to the street.

"I never thought about the exact placement," Frank snicker. "I always take the old shot-gun approach until right now. But if anyone can accomplish exact placement it is a Fencepost. I wonder how much money there is in this?"

The way the scientist end the hour-long demonstration is to say, "The only way the cows on Mr. Carstairs' ranch could produce calves that weren't purebred Charolais is if they were already pregnant."

As Mr. Angstrom promise, he call Frank to the witness chair to have another conversation.

"Now, Mr. Fencepost, would you care to refute any of the testimony you heard Mr. Carstairs give about the day you were fired from your job as ranch foreman?"

"Isn't *refute* the same as garbage?"

"*Refuse* is the same as garbage. *Refute* is . . ."

"Wait a minute. Doesn't r-e-f-u-s-e mean to say you won't do something?"

"In another context r-e-f-u-s-e does mean to turn down an offer . . . to decline . . . Mr. Fencepost, you're good at playing games, are you not?"

"You could say that."

"And could we say that your arranging to get Mr. Carstairs' daughter into bed was a game?"

"It was the one thing Mr. Carstairs warned me to be sure not to do. When you challenge a Fencepost you're asking for a certain amount of trouble."

"But you lost that contest, didn't you?"

"Well, yes and no."

"Meaning?"

"Mr. Carstairs caught us the day he fired me, but that was about the fifty-fifth time in two months that I'd been in her bed. So it looks to me like I'm ahead about fifty-four to one."

"And you were upset about having to run out of the house half dressed, and losing your job, and losing your lover. Is it safe to say that?"

"Pretty safe."

"Now, Mr. Fencepost, since you knew that the cows were in a special pen waiting for Ace Artificial Insemination Inc. to pay their visit, and since the only thing you were forbidden to do, other than callously seduce the boss' daughter, was to let a bull in with the purebred cows, isn't it safe to say that before you left the C Bar C Ranch that day you did the *second* thing you were forbidden to do?"

"You talk a good game," Frank say to Mr. Angstrom. "What if I was to say yes to your last question?"

"It would get my client off the hook, so to speak."

"And it would make Mr. Carstairs even madder at me than he is now?"

"Certainly a possibility."

"And would I be a criminal?"

"You would have played a nasty trick, but as to criminal charges, I am a lawyer, not a judge. I therefore have no opinion on the matter."

Frank consider the situation for a while. "Well, since a Fencepost cannot tell a lie, especially after taking an Indian oath where I'd be struck by lightning before your very eyes . . . yes, I did it."

After the courtroom quiet down Frank continue.

"As I was leaving I seen this here poor old buffalo standing out in the pasture looking sorrowful, and there was eight excited cows in that pen. I said to myself, why shouldn't everybody be happy? And I just let the old buffalo into the cow pen for a couple of hours. As they say, there may be snow on the roof, but there sure was fire in the furnace. By the time I take the buffalo back to pasture, everybody is smiling and . . ."

The judge interrupt Frank to say he's heard enough, and he dismiss the case right there. Ace Artificial Insemination Inc. is off the hook, and Mr. Carstairs is yelling that he going to have buffalo burgers as soon as he gets home to the C Bar C.

Interesting thing is that almost everything Frank said was a lie.

Out on the street, Frank jump in the air like a Russian dancer or a Toyota salesman, try to click his heels together. After he land he give me a high five.

"Confession is good for the soul. Or is it the liver? Anyway, I feel like a great weight been lifted off my shoulders. Honesty is the best policy. Always remember that, Silas."

"Everything you said in there was a lie," I remind him.

"How would you know that?"

"Because I worked on the ranch, too, remember. That afternoon you got chased out of the house, you kept right on going, walk the twelve miles into Camrose on your own. It was after Mr. Carstairs come down to the bunkhouse and fire me for being your friend that I let the buffalo in with the purebred cows."

"Oh. I was wondering how that happened. But I told a good story, didn't I?"

"And after you took an oath."

"Hey, you weren't listening. That was no oath. I was only translating the weather forecast off Channel 2 into Cree. 'Partly cloudy skies and light winds over most of central Alberta, lows tonight in the mid-twenties, highs tomorrow . . .'"

Miracle on Manitoba Street

The second day after we moved into Gorman Tailfeathers' house in The Pit, Frank Fencepost began to work his magic. The Pit is a row of nine old frame houses on a gravel street in an industrial district near the Seattle waterfront. Gorman Tailfeathers is a stocky man of about sixty, with long, gray hair, who work for a bottling plant within walking distance of The Pit — Manitoba Street, as it was officially known.

When I first step out into the yard behind the gaunt, weathered house, where untended lilacs expand over the path to the end of the lot, there are new people moving into the house next door. There is a mother, young daughter, and a red-headed guy about my age. I watch them move in, help the red-headed guy drag a chest of drawers up the back steps, and then up the really narrow stairs to the second floor. The house is laid out exactly the same as the one where me and Frank is visiting.

Back in the yard, as I get used to the sunlight and the overpowering odor of lilac, I see a half-dozen children, all from our house I think; children, grandchildren, nieces, nephews, cousins; running carelessly through the tall grasses, dodging abandoned appliances, stacks of weathered lumber, two skeletal car bodies, one so old it has settled deeply into the earth. A couple of young guys, one with a red bandanna tied across his forehead, lounge on broke-legged lawn chairs, smoking and drinking from unlabeled brown bottles.

A very pretty girl about eighteen, named Ramona, is sitting on the paintless back porch, flicking the ashes from her cigarette into the grasses. She say something that cause the boy with the bandanna to emit a bark-like laugh, and cause the red-headed boy, who told me his name was Tipton, to glance in her direction.

I walk to the end of the lot. Behind a chain-link fence is a graveled acre, soupy from Seattle's continual rain. In the distance I see the fiery interior of a concrete manufacturing plant through twenty-foot-tall open doors. Cement trucks, their cone-shaped hoppers turning ominously, rumble in and out from before dawn until late at night.

There is rhubarb growing along the back fence, a few dead chrome chairs, a soggy mass that once was a mattress, broken bottles, cans, a refrigerator face down like a sleeping drunk.

"Just like home," say Frank as he come into the yard.

Frank is wearing a plaid shirt and faded jeans. His hair brush his shoulders, and he carry in one hand a black felt hat with a row of turquoise and silver conchos around the crown and in his other hand what appear to be a magazine. His face is wide open like a door.

The houses of Manitoba Street are crowded close together like large people in an elevator. Frank make eye contact with the red-headed fellow next door.

Tipton nods hello.

"You new here, hey?" Frank says.

"Yesterday."

"Don't mind these guys," Frank say, nodding toward the fellows on the lawn chairs. "They don't associate with white men. As you can see, they're so successful they already retired to enjoy the fruits of their labors. That one's Fred Horse." He point to the bandanna wearer.

"And Bob Iron Legs." He is a husky fellow in jeans and a denim jacket. "And the guy hiding under the lilacs is my friend, Silas. I'm Frank Fencepost."

Bob Iron Legs snicker loudly. He don't like Frank or me. I think he recognize that Frank is a bigger free-loader than him.

"Tipton Barnes," the red-headed guy says. He ducks around the lilac, steps across a jumble of chicken wire and weeds, and shake Frank's hand.

When he get close he see what Frank holding is actually a small sketch pad. Frank's shirt pocket is crammed with pens and pencils.

"You draw?" Tipton asks.

"Bet your life. One of my many talents. I'm so good at so many things I scare myself."

There is another loud snicker from Bob Iron Legs.

"Want me to show you?" Frank ask. Without waiting for a reply he flip open the sketch pad and, leaning against the splintered doorjamb, begin to sketch the bandanna-wearing Fred Horse.

His hands fly over the page like a hummingbird above a flower.

Suddenly, Frank push the sketch toward Tipton. I wander over to look at it. There is Fred Horse sitting in the broke-backed lawn chair with its twisted aluminum arms. Fred is grinning a cynical grin, the smoke from his cigarette spiraling perfectly. Frank ain't a great artist, but he have ten times my talent, which is limited to stick men.

"That's wonderful," Tipton says.

"If he's so wonderful, why ain't he rich?" says Fred Horse. Bob Iron Legs snickers.

"I got plans," says Frank. It sound almost ominous.

"Me too," says Fred Horse. "Next week, me an' Bob are gonna walk over to Swedish Hospital, perform a little brain surgery."

Both men laugh.

Frank turn to Tipton. "Okay if I draw you?"

"Why not?"

His hand flutter above the paper again. He take longer this time, to impress Tipton.

When he finish he tear off the sheet and hand it to Tipton. It bear him a good but not great resemblance.

"Note," say Frank, "how, though it's drawn in pencil, it capture an eerie quality that leaves no doubt your eyes are blue and your hair red. It's the same with this drawing of Fred, you can tell his bandanna is red."

I sense no such thing. What he capture was that Tipton's front teeth were long and slightly overlapped.

"You can keep it," Frank say.

"Thank you. It's really very good."

"You got a cigarette?"

The pack was bulging in the front pocket of Tipton's shirt. He take out the pack and shake a cigarette in Frank's direction. Frank pull one loose, but eye the half-full pack as if it was raw meat and he was a hungry dog. Tipton push the rest of the pack toward him.

"Even trade," he says, clutching his portrait.

Frank smile. Bob Iron Legs snicker.

Next morning I am sitting on the back steps with Tipton, drinking instant coffee, when Frank slip out the back door clutching his sketch pad.

"Bet you'd like this one," he says to Tipton.

"What is it?" Tipton ask.

Frank sit beside us on the sunny steps. The sketch is of Ramona Blackeye leaning against the splintered doorjamb of the Tailfeathers' house. He capture her shape perfectly, the high cheekbones, her blue jeans, the big-buckled black belt she wear, her blouse tied in a knot across her bare belly.

"Ramona says she likes you," Frank say to Tipton. "She don't understand why you don't make a move on her. She thinks maybe you don't like Indian girls."

"I thought she probably had a boyfriend. I don't want that Bob Iron Legs or one of those other guys on my case."

"You want this?" He push the paper toward Tipton, keeping a tight grip on it while eyeing his shirt pocket.

"This is an almost full pack."

"You think Ramona's sexy, right?"

"Right."

"Okay. I'll give you the sketch free. You give me the cigarettes for the info that she likes you and that's she's unattached."

"Deal."

A little later all three of us is strolling around in Tailfeathers' back yard. Frank is smoking, Tipton is not. Frank stop in front of a dead refrigerator. It is old and stoop-shouldered, weathered a seagull color. The stained enamel is eroding bit by bit, leaving tiny scars that from a distance look like black bugs.

"I've got an idea," says Frank, staring at the refrigerator door.

"Like what?"

"Art. You got to make art where you find it. You got a screwdriver?" he says to Tipton.

"There's one in our house."

"Borrow it to me, and a hammer too. I'll only use them for ten minutes," he go on, noting the skeptical look on Tipton's face.

Tipton walk back to his house and return with a yellow-handled screwdriver and a small hammer. While he's gone Frank sketch something on the refrigerator door in pencil. As soon as Tipton hand him the tools he begin chipping flecks of paint off the door by holding the screwdriver at an angle and tapping the flat end with the hammer.

Flecks of enamel fly. Frank has his eyes squinted almost shut.

"Not bad," he say, as he step back to admire his work.

"What is it?" Tipton asks.

"Step back a little further," Frank says. "You'll see."

We did. And we did. When the distance was right, I could see clear as a photograph what Frank had produced was the face of a woman: not any woman, but what would pass to religious peoples as the Virgin Mary.

"That's pretty good," Tipton says.

"Good enough," says Frank. "Now all we need is have it discovered."

"By who?"

"Somebody who believes in miracles?"

"You planning to pass this off . . . ?"

"Let's let it age for a few days. Help me push this sucker down on its face. The picture need to look as if it's been created by the weather."

"Those guys," I hear Ramona Blackeye telling Tipton, "ain't even cousins of ours. They followed Bob Iron Legs home from a bar down on Pioneer Square. They're Cree from Canada. Traveled down to Montana for a pow-wow and taking the long way home."

What she says is true. Of course, it was Frank's idea to follow Bob Iron Legs home. We sure do thank Gorman Tailfeathers for letting us sleep on his floor.

In the last week Tipton convince Ramona that he *do* like Indian girls. They've spent a couple of interesting afternoons in Ramona's room. Sound really travel in these old houses.

"Silas is okay," Ramona went on, "I sort of rubbed up against him when he first got here, but he has a girlfriend back in Alberta. Frank, on the other hand, thinks he's like one of these holy roller preachers, all he's gotta do is touch a woman on the forehead and she'll flop down on her back."

Ramona's got him pegged perfectly. There are two or maybe three teenage girls that are some relation to the Tailfeathers clan, and Frank share a bed with two of them, maybe all three. I sure get tired of sleeping on the back porch because Frank want his privacy.

Frank spend his early evenings downtown, do some sketch work on the street. He's okay, but not good enough to make more than four or five dollars of an evening. Bob Iron Legs, when he condescend to speak to me, say with what I take to be admiration that Frank know his way around locks. Which I guess is why he came home one night with about twenty cartons of cigarettes and a couple of boxes of melted Popsicles. Frank don't mooch cigarettes from Tipton or me any more, and he help Tipton indirectly by giving Ramona a carton of Winstons, which she shares with him.

"I think Grandma Tailfeathers is the one," Frank say to me about a week later. "She's the head of the house, and she been converted to a Christian when she was girl. She's gonna recognize a picture of the Virgin when she sees one. Trouble is her vision ain't that good."

Grandma Tailfeathers is about four feet nothing, always wears a black dress with a black shawl over her head. She scuffs around in the yard, looking for roots or berries, talks to herself in whatever language she speaks, and whenever she sees Tipton, points his direction with an accusing arthritic finger and says things that I'm certain are not complimentary.

"She's a neat old lady," Ramona says to Tipton one afternoon. "She says I shouldn't be fucking a white man, then asks if you're any good."

Ramona is full-lipped, salmon-colored, and as far as I can tell, totally uninhibited.

"So what did you tell her?"

"I told her the truth," says Ramona obliquely. "Granny says she'd probably fuck a white man, if she could find one as good looking as you."

"I guess that's a compliment," Tipton said.

"Better believe it. So what's Frank up to? He's been sucking up to Granny all week. Keeps crossing himself like a good Catholic, and says he feels the Spirit in the air, something momentous going to happen. He's drawn pictures of Granny Tailfeathers three or four times, always with a halo above her head. I don't like it."

"Today's the day, Brother Tipton," says Frank, when Tipton answer the knock on his door. "If things go according to schedule,

Granny Tailfeathers will be out in the yard in a few minutes, picking rose hips for that brew she keeps stewing on the back of the stove. While she's out there we're gonna upend the fridge and let Granny go nose to nose with the Virgin."

Which is what we do.

"Granny, come here and look at this," Frank say, after I've helped him set the fridge upright. There is mud and little clods of dirt stuck to the fridge door, and there is a small snail about where the Virgin's nose should be.

I'm surprised that Granny comes.

"I don't speak her lingo," says Frank, "but she understands a lot more English than she lets on."

Granny sticks her nose up against the fridge door, but she's so short she's practically looking up the Virgin's nose. She brushes the snail aside, flicks off a couple of clods of dirt.

"Are you thinkin' what I'm thinkin'?" asks Frank.

Granny Tailfeathers studies the image. Ramona ambles sexily down the back steps, and takes Tipton's arm. She gives the Virgin a baleful glance.

"So that's what Frank Shit for Brains has been up to," she says in a stage whisper.

Granny Tailfeathers finally nods her head, turns to Frank, and gives a long, for her, speech in whatever dialect is hers. Then she scuttles off toward the house, her black skirt skimming the grass.

"What did she say?" Frank asks Ramona.

"She says it's a fucking miracle. She's gonna go get a priest."

Frank smiles, showing the large gap in his teeth.

"You could be in serious trouble, asshole," Ramona says.

"This trouble is gonna make us all rich," says Frank. "Especially me."

An hour later Granny come squawking around the corner of the house, pulling a reluctant priest behind her. He looks about sixteen. I didn't know they took them that young.

"What's she want to show me?" the priest say in the direction of Ramona and Tipton. "I can't understand her."

"Take a peek at that fridge," Ramona say, drawing on her Winston.

Frank is lurking like a thief behind the lilac bushes. He take long, loping steps across the yard, arrive at the fridge same time as Granny and the priest.

Once he start to organize things, Frank is as officious as a Banana Republic General. He have us all running errands, spending our own money, which Frank promise faithfully will get replaced when the first visitors start arriving.

We buy some plastic surveyor's tape, flamingo pink. Frank pace off ten feet in each direction and create a circle around the fridge, then he cordon off a pathway from the front of our house, along the really narrow sidewalk down between Tailfeathers' and Tipton's, and up to the circle. I go down to an Army Surplus Store, buy a dozen of those cheap khaki pillows like they rent at ballparks, and he place them in two semicircles in front of the fridge.

"Tipton, my son, my son," Frank says, "I want you to go down to one of those discount stationery stores and buy a roll of brown paper. We going to cover up the inside of the chain link fence, keep people from getting a free view."

Then Frank grin even bigger than usual.

"I'm gonna send three of the little boys out there, give each one a stick and let him poke a hole in the paper. They each charge a dollar to look through the hole. I already checked it out, people won't be able to see nothing but the back of the fridge and the people who paid getting a good look. It will encourage them to come in around the front."

Of course it is Frank who man the entrance. He borrow a card table and a chair from Tipton, set them up close to the sidewalk. Between the table and the path to the back yard he have Bob Iron Legs and Fred Horse standing with their arms folded across their chests, looking mean, just in case somebody think they entitled to sneak a free look at the Virgin.

"First of all," Frank say to everyone come to buy entrance, "I don't think you should go in there. These kinds of thing are always frauds. Hell, anybody could scratch a likeness of the Virgin on a fridge door. All it take is a hammer and a screwdriver and a little bit of talent."

The people all act as if they ain't heard a word Frank said. They just push money at him and ask, "How much?"

"Don't say I didn't warn you. Here's the deal. For two dollars you get a general admission, that takes you within ten feet of the Virgin. You can stay as long as you like, but if you try to get closer, one of my buddies will break your knees. There are about a dozen pillows up closer to the fridge where you kneel and pray. Cost you a dollar a minute."

"I want ten minutes' worth," say a big woman in jeans and yellow sweater, must be at least sixty years old.

Frank take a piece of sticky note paper, look at his watch. "It's 6:15 now," he say. He write 6:25 on the paper, stick it on the back pocket of the woman's jeans.

"One of our attendants will tap you on the shoulder when your time is up. Have a good prayer." And he send the woman on her way. "You want to buy more time, you got to come back here," he yells after her. "The attendants ain't allowed to take your money."

Turns out most people want to go inside the circle. Next day we up the number of cushions to twenty and often still have a little line-up. One time two ladies get into a real hair-puller over who was to get the next available prayer cushion.

Then word come down that a delegation from the Catholic church, including a couple of four-star-general types, are on their way to take a look at the Virgin.

"I was a virgin once," Ramona says to Tipton. "I should have got this kind of attention."

"I wonder if we should let them in?" says Frank to no one in particular.

"If they approve, the crowds will increase," I say.

"If they approve, guess who'll be out on the street like garbage, and who'll be raking in the dough?"

The newspapers and television people refer to what's happening as The Miracle on Manitoba Street, snooping around asking questions or filming the line-up of people waiting to kneel in front of the refrigerator.

Frank have this theory that you don't have to know what you doing, that you only have to look the part. That seem to apply to the Virgin of the Refrigerator. Me and Frank and our friends know the whole operation is phony. The people who come must suspect it is phony, but they want really badly to believe, so they pay their money, pray their prayers, and come away believing their arthritis or back pain or blurred vision has been cured by the Virgin. Scary.

Frank suggest early on that we pay one of the Tailfeathers clan, preferably Gorman, to enjoy a miraculous cure and witness to the TV and newspapers, but we don't have to. Big women in cheap clothes and out-of-style hair-dos babble in tongues and come away from the refrigerator claiming their epilepsy has been cured, or their insides untangled, and one lady claim she reduced thirty pounds right on the spot. The crowd is about 90 percent women and children, and what few men there are appear to have been dragged along by a wife or mother.

"I wonder why women are more eager for miracles than men?" says Frank. "And what kind of miracle would appeal to men? Silas, I'm gonna have to look into that."

The TV confirm that some Catholic cardinal flying all the way from New York to Seattle next week, and they speculate that he going to view the Virgin on the Refrigerator.

That night Granny call a big meeting in Tailfeathers' living room. There are more people living in the house than I imagined. Ramona does the translating for Granny Tailfeathers, who gets right to the point by saying she wants her cut of the profits.

"One for all, and all for one, is the way I see things," says Frank.

Granny say it is the all for one aspect she don't like, especially since she suspect the *one* is Frank.

"Whoa! You must think I'm made of money here," says Frank. "I got expenses. I been paying Bob and Fred as guards, Ramona and Tipton enforce the praying time, Silas here run errands. There ain't much profit."

Granny let loose a long mouthful of Indian words.

"Granny says you're full of shit," says Ramona. "She seen you make the picture on the fridge. She wants to rent a Winnebago and visit her sisters in Montana before she dies."

Ramona pause, listen to Granny again. "She also wants one of them twenty-eight-inch TVs for the living room, a washer and dryer set, an electric can opener, and a deepfreezer full of buffalo meat."

Frank is in the middle of the room, and there ain't very many friendly eyes looking at him. He been using for a pillow an Albertson's grocery store shopping bag, stuffed fat with ten- and twenty-dollar bills. He have the bag under his jean jacket right now.

"How could you even think I wasn't gonna share with my brothers and sisters, and Granny," he say, smiling at the old woman who is all angles like she's made out of coat hangers. "If you was to make me divide up the money right now, why we could do that. But, I'd be forced to confess to the TV people that I drawed the face on the fridge. As I see it we got maybe another week before (a) that cardinal put the kibosh on our little gold mine, and (b) people just generally get tired of the whole idea."

Frank go on for about fifteen minutes, and by the time he's finished he convinced everybody that he is really doing them a favor by acting as banker, and as soon as the incoming money slow down to a trickle, why it will all get divided up properly.

Even Granny seem to be sucked in.

In another week the rush is over. Hardly any new people coming to see the Virgin, but there is a group of faithful come every day with ten or twenty dollars, like people who go to an arcade or a bingo hall every chance they get. The story about the cardinal coming to see our Virgin turn out not to be true. He did come to Seattle, but not to see us.

Frank send me downtown to buy us first-class seats to Edmonton. "Tell them we want pretty flight attendants and lots of them After Eight chocolates," he say, as I heading off.

"Night after next we going to divide things up," Frank promise.

"I think that same night the fridge get destroyed by vandals. Who wants to be a vandal?" Frank ask, and quite a few hands go up.

"Sleep light," Frank say to me. "We'll sneak out about dawn."

The racket happen quite a bit sooner. At 4:00 a.m. the lights is all on, and the room fill up with half-dressed Indians and men in brown uniforms.

"Immigration and Naturalization," says one of the men, holding up identification with one hand, a nasty-looking gun in the other. "We have reason to believe there are illegal aliens here."

Who would have done this to us?

"We are citizens of the world," Frank explain, but it don't seem to do no good.

Me and Frank turn out to be the only illegal aliens at Tailfeathers' house.

"Hey, we got tickets to go home in just a few hours," Frank say.

"Okay, we'll just give you a ride to the airport and see that you use them," the Immigration guy says.

Now Frank is in a spot. He can't very well take along an Albertson shopping bag full of cash.

As we being marched out the back door, I see Granny Tailfeathers, grinning where her teeth used to be, imagining, I bet, that she zooming across the prairie in her rented Winnebago.

The Elevator

A beat-up red Fargo truck with a flatdeck and one green fender pull into Fred Crier's Hobbema Texaco garage one evening early in July. It is easy to see that the driver, a man about thirty, is the type who is happy when covered in grease. His gray railroad coveralls are oily, he have black smears on his face and arms, and even though he is white his hands is darker than mine, the nails chipped and black.

"You lookin' for a job?" he says, when he sees me leaning against the building taking in a little sun.

"What kind?" I say.

"Got a demolition job up in the Peace River country. I'm drivin' straight through."

He names the wages.

"A month or so's work and a bus ticket back. How about it?"

"Why not?" I say. "I ain't been off the reserve for a while."

The trucker's name is Gil, and all night we take turns driving. About dawn we pull in at a truck stop somewhere past Whitecourt, and in the café there, Gil talk another young Indian into coming with us.

The new guy's name is Leonard and he is skinny and shy. After I ask him quite a few times, he tell me he is Dog Rib come from someplace forever north of us.

About mid-morning we turn off the highway, drive on gravel for a couple of hours, then on a dirt road run parallel to the railway tracks. Gil finally stop at what look like a town. But when I get out of the truck I can see that nobody lives at this place any more.

"My boss got himself the contract to tear this down," Gil says, as we walk toward a tall, spooky-looking grain elevator.

I don't know what I expected; rows and rows of big sheet-metal pipes or some kind of compartments where grain could be stored. But whatever I thought, the whole inside had been gutted. It is cool and hollow, smell of musty grain and mice.

Our voices echo like we was talking into an oil drum. A pigeon flutters off a ledge up high, scared by our talking, and escapes through a hole only it can see. A single feather floats down, taking a long time in the heavy air.

There are ladders nailed against each wall, and it is so far up that they narrower at the top than at the bottom. Gil give us each a hammer and a small crowbar.

Leonard, he hook his crowbar in his belt and give the wall a thump with his hammer. When he do that a cloud of dust leap out of the wall like it was waiting to be released. I had taken off my shirt outside, and that dust settle into my hair and stick to my damp back and shoulders. The sound the hammer make is muffled, as if Leonard held a blanket against the wall and hit into it.

"You start at the top," Gil says.

Me and Leonard both bend back our necks and look way up to the hollow made by the peaked roof.

"You climb up the ladders," Gil go on. "First thing to do is hammer a hole in the roof. You toss the loose boards and shingles to the ground. When you get a good pile, you come down and make a neat stack. I'll be around every second day or so for a new load."

While we worked, Gil drove to wherever the closest town was and bought us each a thin green bedroll and a sheet of mosquito netting. That night we spread out the bedrolls in the long grass next to the elevator and hope it don't rain. Guess that is why they hire Indians to do this work. White men gonna want to be put up in a hotel or at least a bunkhouse.

This is about the quietest place I've ever been. Across the street is three houses and a tall building with a false front, have "General Store" painted on it in black letters that is pretty much faded. The buildings have all their glass busted away. No matter how far from civilization a place is, there is always somebody around to bust out the windows.

Grass and weeds peek in the lowest windows of the houses, so when the wind blows I can hear them ticking and swishing against the siding even when I am way up the elevator. The street, which never been anything but dirt, is now growed over by pigweed and creeping charlie. Thousands of dandelions bloom yellow as lemon candies.

In one of the houses Gil store a big box of canned food, a can opener, and a case or three of pop. There is an old well with a rusty pump out behind the elevator.

Every second day, regular as a clock, Gil show up with a new box of supplies. All three of us load the flatdeck truck with lumber, chain it on, and away Gil goes, the truck grumbling off in compound low gear.

The roof of the elevator is gone by now, and we worked down about three feet all the way around. Only the ladders stick over the top, look like a picture I seen once of how someone tried to build a tower all the way to heaven.

I bet we been there ten days already when I notice that even though the elevator stand right beside the railroad tracks, there has never been even one train go by.

I wonder, did the elevator die first or did the train stop running and kill off the elevator?

During the daytime the sky is a glaring blue, and the poplars along the right-of-way look black when the afternoon sun is behind them. Now that we worked the elevator down a few more feet, we are right out in the open and our hammering sound like gun shots, and the crowbar pulling nails make noises like something in pain, frightening the songbirds into silence.

The way I meet old Standing-in-the-bush, is because I got a good nose, and because I am hungry for coffee.

Leonard and me kind of enjoy sleeping out in the tall grass. The air is fresh and sweet and cool, but I sure miss not being able to cook up coffee.

"It is cruelty to poor Indians not to give us coffee in the mornings," I say to Leonard.

He just smile shy and crack open a bottle of 7-Up.

I make myself a cheese sandwich and crank up some water with the old iron pump. It is while I'm drinking down the water that I smell pine smoke.

"I didn't know there was anybody living close by," I say.

I figure where there's pine smoke on a July morning there must be a stove cooking coffee. I just follow the smell and sure enough about a half mile down the railroad grade and about a hundred yards back in a clearing sit a little log cabin. The cabin have pigweed growing tall off the flat roof. The cracks between logs have been plastered with mud, just like we do at home. There are two small sheds in the yard and a corral hold a few cattle.

I knock on the screen door and try to see into the cabin, but I can't because of the way sunlight shine on the screen. There is a leather and sour milk smell in the air around the door.

From inside, a very old voice say to me in Cree, "Are you one of my grandchildren?"

A yellow dog come around the corner of the cabin, crawl on its belly, whine in a friendly way.

"No. I work up the road aways. I hoped you might have a cup of coffee to spare."

I been able to smell that coffee cooking for a long ways, the odor so spicy it make my mouth water.

"You speak Cree like a white man," say the voice, "and you smell of the city. I can smell beer and store food."

"I ain't had a beer for over a week or more."

"The odor stays on your skin," the voice say, and the screen door push open.

The doorstep is made out of two hewed logs, and big blue flies buzz around in the sunshine.

An old man in soft moccasins shuffle out, his knees stiff as if they been glued in straight.

"I am Standing-in-the-bush," he say. "How do you call yourself?"

"Silas Ermineskin."

"You are one of the ones tearing down the white man's big colored box," and he laugh, a soft, throaty sound. "They collect food up to the sky, but deep in the winter, when my cattle were hungry, they would not share."

He shake his head and motion for me to come inside the cabin, which smell of closed air and medicines. As my eyes become accustomed to the dark I see roots and leaves hanging on strings criss-crossed from wall to wall.

Standing-in-the-bush won't take no money for his coffee, which he pour for me from a tall gray-enameled pot that live on the back of his cookstove like a pet. While we drink, I find out that the town was called Frog Pond, but was never big enough to really be a town, get a post office, a gas pump, or even its name on the side of the elevator.

"Even the frog pond is gone," says Standing-in-the-bush. And he tell me how the place where me and Leonard sleep at night used to have thousands and thousands of frogs sing so loud they could be heard for miles on a summer night.

"When I was young and rode out at night to steal horses, we always hoped our enemies were camped by a frog swamp. Frogs have evil spirits, their noise clogs the ears. Once, I crawled right into an enemy camp and untied three ponies, and led them away." Standing-in-the-bush laugh softly again, showing a couple of bent, yellow teeth.

After I tell Leonard what Standing-in-the-bush has told me, he say, "So even the evil spirits have moved away from this place."

That is the most words Leonard has spoke since we been here.

Standing-in-the-bush invite me back the next morning. When I go, I take with me from our supplies a tin of peaches and a package of Export A cigarettes to leave in payment for my coffee.

It is three more days before I meet Simon. I am at the top of the elevator, banging loose first a board from the outside, then a board from the inside, when from far down the dusty road that run parallel to the rusted railroad tracks where saplings and thistles grow up between the rotting ties, I see a tall, stoop-shouldered man walking toward me. He is walking with his hands up like someone was pointing a gun at him, each hand closed on the end of a pole, the middle of which rests on the back of his neck. He wears baggy overalls so dirty and greasy look as if they might stand on their own if the man was to step out of them.

When he gets even with the elevator, he swing the pole down off his shoulder, look up at me and wave his hand.

"Mighty hot," he says. "Can you spare a drink?"

"Got a choice of cold water or warm pop," I holler down.

He take off his cap, pump some water over his head, then cup his hands and take a good big drink. His face is long, his eyes deep set, his forehead high and iron-colored. He got hollow cheeks and his gray hair is brushcut. His nose look cut from rock, just brown skin glued tight to bone.

He wave thank you and go on his way. I notice that the pole was not a pole, but a piece of metal pipe with some kind of holder on the top end. If I didn't know better I would think it was a speaker post from a drive-in theater.

Next morning when I go for coffee I find that same man sitting at Standing-in-the-bush's table. First thing I notice is his hands would make two of mine, the veins on the back make them look rough as spruce bark.

"This is Simon," says Standing-in-the-bush. "He already forgot his Indian name and take one like yours from the white man's book."

He don't say that with meanness, just repeating a fact he can't do nothing about.

A while later Standing-in-the-bush say, "The white man want to give me a name." He is smiling a crook-toothed smile from under a red cap have big earflaps on it. "When I won't pick one, they give me one. 'I am Standing-in-the-bush,' I say, when I go to collect my treaty money, and when I sign up to homestead my land.

" 'Which one?' they want to know.

" 'The only one,' I tell them.

"But they hand on me George. When white men live in the houses up the road, they call me George. For forty years they wonder why I don't answer them."

Simon mainly stay quiet, drink black coffee, smoke cigarettes, suck his lower lip in against his teeth.

"Simon lives up the road," Standing-in-the-bush says, waving his hand back in the direction of the elevator. He work thirty years for the drive-in theater. Paint their fence, repair the talking boxes that stand on sticks in their big yard."

"Drive-in?" I say, surprised. It seems to me I am somewhere in the middle of the wilderness.

"Um-hm," says Simon.

"There's a good sized town eight miles up the road, other small towns, lots of farmers and Indians. Now everybody got the talking pictures in their houses, don't have to go out no more."

"Um-hm," says Simon again, almost smile, but not quite.

"Three years ago, about the time the drive-in theatre closed up forever, a car come driving into my yard, filled with men in suits and a priest. I figured they was planning to take me away like they did to some other old people.

"So I point my gun at them and make them go away.

"After that the mounties come around banging at my door, so I ease myself into the bush and live in the hills for a summer. The winter mounties don't come looking for me. White men have poor memories and no patience.

"I was here when they built the first railroad," Standing-in-the-bush go on. "I don't know how much I remember and how much my mama told me. The men from the railroad used to come to our camps along the river. They make our men go with them to work on the railroad.

"'They work them like horses, from sun to sun,' my mother told me. The white men were given money, but our men were paid cheap wine in wooden barrels. They would roar like beasts, crash through the bush, do harm to their families and each other. Then the white men would come back with their guns, and take them away, dirty, reeking, trembling, to work again laying down the iron river.'"

Behind Standing-in-the-bush's cabin, Simon keep a stock of those metal posts from the drive-in theater. Some of them have the big, square-headed speakers attached, some don't. Simon have cans of paint, silver and black, for painting the posts and speakers. The air is sharp with their scent.

"He lives up there now in the building where they used to sell food," the old man says.

"Um-hm," agree Simon.

It is about this time I begin to catch on that Simon is working for Simon these days, not for the drive-in theater.

The elevator is now only about thirty feet tall. Gil truck away the lumber fast as we pile it up.

"Everything is changing for the worse," says Standing-in-the-bush. "Only Simon tries to make things better."

"The white man's colored pictures get in the blood like whiskey," says Simon, pulling in his lower lip real hard.

Another time he talk a little. We all three sit on the log steps, smoking, watch the sun set into the muskeg.

"I had an old lady one time," says Simon. "Name was Gladys. She was pretty. Grew her hair down to where I could tuck the ends in the back pockets of her jeans.

"Not much to keep a pretty woman here. At first she liked to watch the colored movies every summer night, but then she wanted to live like in the movies. Whenever my pay checks come, she go to town, sit in the bar, drink beer, smoke tailor-made cigarettes. 'Get drunk and be somebody,' is what she used to say.

"Guess one time she really got to be somebody. She disappeared. There was oil drillers around. I sort of expected her to come back when times got tough. But I guess they never did. I guess she's still somebody.

"The boys, Alex and Rufus, was little then, no place to leave them while I was at work so I sent them to live with Gladys' sister down in Peace River. I always meant to go see them . . .

"Maybe they got kids of their own, now . . . "

Next morning a short man with a round belly hid under a vest and a forehead like pink washboard come around give us our pay in cash. Near as I can figure he don't cheat us, pay us the money we earn without none of those deductions the government ordinarily steal from us. That probably mean that whoever is paying him or his company to tear down the elevator is paying cash too, so they can't ask about where the lumber end up. On our first day here Gil tell us, "If anybody come around asking questions about what you're doing or who you work for, you don't know nothing."

"About what?" I say, and we both smile big.

The pink-faced man stare up at the elevator, which is now only about fifteen feet high, with ladders peeking over all four sides, like snakes trying to escape.

"Be ready to roll in the morning," he says. "You can ride to Whitecourt with Gil. He'll give you bus money from there."

He take a roll of bills from his back pocket and pay us our last day's wages.

"How come you keep repairing things at the drive-in theater?" I ask Simon the next morning, as the three of us drinking our last coffee together. It is blinding hot already, and the sky is hazy as if there was a forest fire close around.

"I don't want it to change," says Simon. "I don't want it to go back to bush like the railroad."

"He carries sacks of gravel down there, he grades the little hills where the cars used to line up beside the talking boxes. He had to move in 'cause kids used to drive out at night roar their cars around that big lot. Sometimes when the clouds were right I could see the colored pictures reflected off them. I used to peek through the fence sometimes. I seen cowboys fighting Indians, and people dancing."

Simon walks around behind the cabin and returns with a silver speaker pole resting across his shoulders and neck, then he hooks his arms up behind so the pole almost becomes part of him.

"You figure if you keep things up the white man going to bring his colored pictures back one day?" the old man say very slowly.

"Um-hm," says Simon, staring at his feet. "I can hope."

Standing-in-the-bush turns to stare across the clearing and corral to the scrub poplars standing all fluttery-leafed in the hot July wind.

"Don't do no harm to dream," the old man says.

"I'll dream those movies back," says Simon. "Everything's painted and in better shape than when they quit it. They'll be surprised when they come to open up again."

"You see your movies on that big white screen," says the old man, "sometimes when I look far away, I dream of the buffalo. I must be the only one who remembers them. I liked the train, but it went away. I liked the movies. Sometimes they made the earth tremble just like the buffalo."

They are standing almost back to back, Simon shaped like a cross staring off toward his immaculate theater, Standing-in-the-bush gazing across his corral where two skinny roan steers reach their necks through the poles for grass.

Ice Man

"**I**s that kid Jason Twelve Trees here again?" Ma says, as she look across the table to where he's sitting between me and my brother Joseph. "I'm gonna adopt him. Might as well make him an Ermineskin, he lives here most of the time anyway."

We can tell Ma is joking, but it is true that Jason Twelve Trees spend a lot of his time at our house. It is my littlest sister Delores who is the attraction. They ain't old enough to be sweethearts, though, if Delores ever gonna have a sweetheart, I guess I know who it's gonna be.

Jason Twelve Trees like being around Delores because she is about as independent as a sixth-grade girl ever gonna get. Delores' hair is long and blue-black. Ma says she always looks as if she just came in out of a wind storm. Delores got a three-cornered tear in her jeans and a toe poking out of one sneaker. She wear a green T-shirt that say "Kiss Me I'm an Indian," and has a dimple that twinkles when she smiles. Her eyes are brown as polished furniture and her nose wide, with a few freckles.

Delores collect empty bottles from all over the reserve and along the ditches of Highway 2. She earn her genuine chicken-dancer costume that way. Delores won many a blue ribbon at pow-wows in Alberta and Saskatchewan, and she dance regular at the Calgary Stampede and at Klondike Days in Edmonton with Molly Thunder's dance troupe, call themselves the Duck Lake Massacre.

Jason Twelve Trees like to hang around me, too. He sit at the kitchen table and talk while I'm trying to type my stories.

"You know, Silas, you and Delores get to do what you want to with your lives. My dad wants me to be something I don't want to be."

"And what's that?"

Jason's family live in a new housing project on the east side of the reserve. His dad is a mechanic who worked at the Texaco station in Wetaskiwin for about ten years, then take over the building where a Petro Canada station died and open up a three-bay auto repair shop that has done real well. The Twelve Trees got two telephones in their house, and their phones don't ever get cut off.

"My dad thinks I plot everything I do just to bug him," Jason say. "He thinks I could like mechanics if I wanted to. Life would sure be a lot simpler if I could."

Jason Twelve Trees is slim and coffee-colored, have his hair pretty long. His shirt is clean, even though this is probably the second day he's worn it.

"'Jay,' my dad's always saying, 'You ought to be in pig heaven. When I was your age I'd have killed to have a real garage to work in any time I wanted. We've got almost every tool known to the auto industry. When I was a kid I used to go to the auto wreckers in Wetaskiwin, beg for a busted carburetor I could tinker with.'

"Then Dad tells me how he saved the money he earned from pitching hay for some white farmer to buy a set of wrenches. 'Jay, I can't describe the feeling as I laid down my money and reached out to touch those beautiful silver tools. I wanted to cry I was so happy.'

"I try to argue, Silas, but it don't do me much good. 'What if Grandpa Twelve Trees had wanted you to be a rancher or a truck driver?' I ask.

"'I'd have become a mechanic,' Dad says. 'I was born to be a mechanic. And I'm waiting for the day I can change the sign to *Twelve Trees & Son Automotive*. If you'd just give it a try you'd get the feel for it, son.'

"But I ain't got a mechanical bone in my body."

"It's your life," I say absently, erasing another strikeover.

"But you know what probably bugs my dad worse than anything?"

I shake my head.

"My best friend being a girl."

Then he tell me, again, about how him and Delores stopped by his dad's shop, and how Delores dove right in and helped make some repairs and ended up covered in grease.

"When they finished the car repairs my dad said, 'Maybe Jason will make us lunch?'

"It didn't come out funny."

The idea Jason's dad can't seem to get a handle on is that he wants to be a chef.

"I can't seem to get across to my dad that I know *exactly* how he felt when he bought his first set of wrenches. It is kind of like we belong to different branches of the same religion, but won't listen to each other.

"When our kindergarten class visited the kitchen at the McDonald's restaurant in Wetaskiwin, I stared up at all that stainless steel. Everything was so white and bright. So clean. And the kitchen smelled so good. The cooks moved fast and sure seemed to be enjoying what they were doing. I decided right then and there that I was going to be a cook.

"Mom lets me help her in the kitchen, but Dad hates it, so Mom and I don't tell when I've helped with dinner, even if I cooked it myself with hardly any help."

Ma sympathize with Jason. She even asks questions that let him show off what he knows.

"You can do anything you've got the ambition to do," is what Ma's always told me and Illianna and all the rest of us kids.

Jason's face light up.

"Go out and meet life head-on," Ma tells us, "instead of hanging around waiting for life to come to you."

The first time Jason went to the kitchen of the restaurant in the new Wetaskiwin shopping mall, "I peeked in the back door," he said. "The cooks all looked like angels in their white jackets and tall white hats. There was so much bustle it remind me of Mad Etta's cabin that time you took me over to watch her boil up roots and leaves to make medicine.

"I must have stood there for an hour until the owner, Mr. Nick, came out to get some air. Nick is his first name. His last name is Greek and have about forty letters.

"'Mr. Nick,' I said, 'I want to work in your kitchen.'

"'What do you figure you could do in there?' he asked.

"I thought of the things I did to help my mother at home.

"'I . . . I could dry dishes,' I said. 'I could scrape plates. I could take out the garbage, peel carrots and potatoes, and I'm careful not to make the peelings too thick . . .'

"'Sounds like you'd be better than some of these guys. How old are you?'

"'Almost eleven,' I said.

"'You're Merton Twelve Trees' boy, aren't you?'

"'Yes.'

"'Well, you've got a few years before I can put you on the payroll, but come have a look around.'

"I bet I asked Mr. Nick a thousand questions. He invited me to come back any time."

And Jason did. I bet he could fill in for just about anybody but the head chef.

First ice sculpture Jason Twelve Trees saw was at Mr. Nick's restaurant. I was there with him. The restaurant was closed that day because Mr. Nick was catering a Greek wedding.

"Where's Mr. Nick?" Jason asked Stavros, the head chef, who was chopping squid, one eye on a cauldron of lemon-smelling soup.

"In the cooler," said Stavros.

When we opened the door to the cooler a flood of cold air rushed out like steam. Mr. Nick was standing with his back to us, a wooden packing case in front of him.

"What are you doing?" Jason asked.

Mr. Nick stepped to one side and there on the packing case was the biggest ice-fish I ever seen. It must have been four feet long and looked alive, curving as if he was leaping above the water of a lake.

Mr. Nick wore a white smock over his suit and held a glinting blue chisel in his hand. Other chisels and pointy silver tools lay on a piece of wine-colored velvet on the packing box.

"How do you like him?" Mr. Nick asked. "Caught him myself," he laughed.

"Did you make that?" Jason asked.

"How else," said Mr. Nick. "It's a table decoration for the buffet. You want to help me carry this one down to the freezer? Then you can help carry another block of ice up here. I'm going to carve a wedding cake with a bride and groom on top."

"Wow! Making things out of ice," Jason said.

I had never realized how beautiful ice could be.

As Mr. Nick worked on the new block of sparkling blue ice he explained the uses of each tool. Some of them were obvious, the tongs, the handsaw, the drill, a coarse-grained rasp, the calipers and dividers for measuring. But the flat, angle, and curved chisels, the six-point chippers, the one-point chipper — Mr. Nick said these were like an artist's brushes, everyone used them in a very personal way according to how they saw the world.

It was hard to find a store that sold ice-carving tools. Mr. Nick had brought his from the old country. Jason looked through restaurant supply catalogs until he found a place in Edmonton that stocked them.

"I'm going to make some ice sculptures," Jason said to Delores as we were driving up Highway 2.

"What?"

"It's something that a chef has to know. Some people carve things out of stone? I'm going to make them with ice."

"Etta say the form is there already," I say. "If you have the gift you'll be able to knock away whatever is covering it."

"I sure hope I have the gift," said Jason.

At the restaurant supply store there were aisles and aisles of shining dishes, glasses, and stainless steel kitchen equipment.

"I'd like some ice-carving tools," Jason said, swallowing hard.

The chisels and choppers were displayed on a background of midnight-blue velvet. They were a lot more expensive than I imagined.

"If you decide you don't want these any more," the salesman said, as he wrapped them up, "I'll buy them back at half price."

"Oh, no," said Delores. "He's going to be a chef. He'll always need these tools."

Friday afternoon we bought two blocks of ice from the machine at the Wetaskiwin shopping mall, wrapped them in gunnysack and stashed them in the freezer in the Twelve Trees' basement. When his mom and dad went shopping, Jason and Delores got one of the blocks from the freezer and set it on the workbench.

Jason's new tools glowed like surgical instruments under the bright light.

He blew on the clear, bluey ice and watched the little puff of frosty air bounce back toward him. He picked up a chisel, trying to decide where to start.

"We could go for a walk if we make you too nervous," I said.

"No, it's okay," Jason said. "See, I'm going to try and turn this block of ice into a hen sitting on a nest, like this little ornament of my mom's, and like the picture I've drawn here."

He took a felt pen and haltingly traced the outline of the template on the block of ice.

He placed the chisel against the ice and tapped it gently with a rubber-headed mallet.

An hour later we were all shivering. Jason's and Delores' clothes were soaked. The block of ice had shrunk. Jason's chiseling and chipping had revealed a form, but it didn't look much like a hen sitting on a nest.

"I wasn't expecting much first try," Jason said. "But I was expecting a little more than this."

We were still mopping up the basement floor when Jason's folks came home, so I explained about the ice sculpture.

Jason's dad looked amused. I guess he figured making art out of ice beat cooking. I don't think he ever connected the two, so Jason didn't make any secret about practicing ice sculpture in the basement.

After about twenty blocks of ice Jason started to turn out recognizable forms: a bird, a car, a big fish, and that hen sitting on a nest.

"Some evenings," he'd tell Delores, "my dad comes to look at what I'm doing. 'How come you want to make art out of something that turns to slush in a few hours?' he asks.

"I had to think about that for a minute.

"'All the cars you repair eventually end up in the junkyard,' I said.

"'That's different,' said my dad. But I couldn't see the difference.

"Another time he said, 'You know, I think you're getting better. Maybe we can get you art lessons. Then you could use *real* materials.'"

One day an announcement appeared on the bulletin board next to the principal's office at Jason's school.

CITY OF WETASKIWIN
RECREATION COMMISSION
COOKING
COMPETITION
For GIRLS 12-16
Soups • Salads
Appetizers
Entrees • Desserts

He read the notice over and over, then copied down how to get an entry form.

Jason told Delores about the poster, showed her what he'd copied down, and said, "That contest should be for boys, too. Don't they realize some boys like to cook?"

"So call them on it," said Delores. "The Baseball Association had to be hit over the head before they realized that some girls like to play baseball."

"How could I call them on it?"

"There're two ways," said Delores. "The first would be to get yourself an entry form, cook whatever you want and enter it. J. Twelve Trees could be either a boy or a girl. Or," and she looked at me kind of sideways, "you just call up that lady at City Hall, that Mrs. Duvall whose name is on the poster, and tell her you want to enter the contest. She might not give you any trouble."

"What if she does?"

"Then you go to somebody higher, and somebody higher after that. If it gets tough, tell them bias goes against the Constitution. That's the way I got to play baseball."

But everybody gave him trouble.

"As the poster clearly states," Mrs. Duvall said when Jason got her on the phone, "the contest is for girls only. The Commission also sponsors a dog show . . . maybe you could enter your dog."

"I want to enter the cooking contest," Jason said, stubbornly.

"I'm afraid that won't be possible."

Jason cleared his throat. "Mrs. Duvall, could I please speak to your supervisor?"

The supervisor's name was either Perkins or Parkins. He said the same thing as Mrs. Duvall, only he was firmer about it.

"If we made an exception for you, why just anybody could enter."

"I don't want you to make an exception for me," Jason said. "*Anybody* between twelve and sixteen *should* be able to enter."

"Quite impossible," said Mr. Perkins-Parkins. "I'm awfully busy, little boy." And he hung up.

"They sounded fairly polite," said Delores. "You should have been there when I tackled the Baseball Association."

That night there was a baseball game. The league is for ten- to fourteen-year-olds, and the teams are sponsored by local businesses.

Delores is better than the worst players, but nowhere near a star, but I like to watch her when she's at bat. She gets a fierce look in her eye, and her tongue peeks from the corner of her mouth. She's not very fast on the bases, but she runs with purpose. Instead of hitting the inside corner of the bag at first, the way the coach teaches, Delores plunks her foot right in the middle of the base, which takes a little extra time.

Delores used to hang around the baseball field, chase foul balls, until one night when the Little Buffaloes was short a player. Mr. Oldfield, the coach, said to Delores, "How would you like to play left field tonight?"

But as soon as she took the field the opposing coach went running out to the umpire.

"That's a girl," he said, pointing to left field. "Girls aren't allowed in this league." And he ruffled through a sheaf of papers until he found the rule that said the league was only for boys.

The umpire ruled that Delores couldn't play.

"Well, we'll see about that," said Ma.

Ended up there was a meeting of all the coaches and the team sponsors where Delores got to make a little speech about how much she enjoyed playing baseball, and how she didn't care whether she played with boys or girls, and why should anyone else? With only a couple of exceptions, everyone agree with her, and this year there's a dozen girls playing, at least one on every team.

Things weren't as simple when Jason decided to challenge the rules of the Recreation Commission.

"We should threaten to get a lawyer," I said. "The City don't want any trouble with lawyers. I bet they'll back down right away."

But I was wrong.

The local newspaper got hold of the story. They sent a photographer and a reporter around to Jason's house. The next day there was his photograph under a headline that said: WOULD-BE COOK CHALLENGES RECREATION COMMISSION.

"How could you embarrass me like this?" Jason's father come steaming up to our cabin looking for Jason.

"I have to face my friends," his father went on. "I'll have to admit I have a son who wants to enter a girls' cooking contest."

"But that's the whole point," Jason said. "*Anybody* should be able to enter that contest."

His father just glared at him.

The guys at his school were twice as bad.

"It's not worth it," Jason said that evening after supper.

"You can still quit, Jason," Ma said. "Though I took you for the kind of kid who might enjoy being a pioneer."

"I do like the idea," Jason said. "Me and Delores being first ones to . . ."

". . . fight off the Indians," said Delores.

"But I've got the Indians on my side, so I can't lose, right?" said Jason.

"Right," said Delores and Ma.

Thinking about the hearing at Wetaskiwin City Hall was one thing, being there was another. The three City Commissioners resent being there. They all have regular jobs; one is a bank manager, one runs the United Grain Growers elevator, and the other owns a car dealership. The City of Wetaskiwin is represented by their lawyer.

Jason have Mad Etta, our medicine lady.

"I'm kind of doctor, lawyer, Indian chief, all rolled into one," says Etta.

But when it come to sitting down all by himself at the hearing, Jason is glad to have any company, even Etta.

"Hmmph," say Etta, stare right through that lawyer fellow. Then she sort of puff herself up, like a prairie chicken, seem to get quite a bit bigger than she already is. She reach across and hold one of Jason's hands.

Jason makes his case by bringing up the Charter of Rights and Freedoms, and the Constitution. He reading from notes been given to him by our friend Bedelia Coyote. My guess is the lawyer for Wetaskiwin don't know if Jason is bluffing or not. I have a mixed-up feeling about what Jason is doing. I figure from reading the newspapers that only crooks and illegal immigrants use the Charter of Rights.

"The City Commissioners will make a decision later this afternoon or this evening," the lawyer for the City say to Jason. "Someone will call you at home."

"He'll be at my house, where there ain't no phone," Delores said. "With a lot of friends," and she dig Jason in the ribs with her elbow.

It was Jason's mother turn up at our door that evening.

"Did I win?"

"Well, let's say you won and you lost. Do you know what a compromise is?"

"When each side of an argument gives in a little, but not too much?"

"That's about right. The Recreation Commission decided that from now on their cooking contest will be open to both boys and girls. But, they said, this year's competition was too far along to change the rules. So you won't be able to enter the contest until next year."

"That's okay," he said.

"I got my idea playing second base," Jason told us later. "There was a runner on first and the batter hit a hard grounder to me. I fielded it on two bounces and tossed to the shortstop covering second. He leapt in the air to avoid the sliding runner and threw to first for the double play. What froze in my mind was the picture of the shortstop in mid air, his arm cocked to fire the ball, the runner sliding under his feet.

"As soon as school was over, I phoned Mrs. Duvall. She sniffed and said very coldly, 'What can I do for you now?'

"'I'd like to volunteer to do something else,' I said.

"'And what's that?'

"'There's no competition for ice carving, is there?'

"'What do you mean?'

"'Ice sculpture. I'd like to decorate the tables with ice carvings the day of the competition.'

"There was a long silence. I guess she was trying to figure out if it was a trick.

"'That's very nice of you, Jason,' Mrs. Duvall said, her voice softer, 'I think that would be a lovely idea. I'll have to run it by the board of directors, but I'm sure it will be fine.'"

"Alright!" Delores yelled.

Jason started practicing the next day in the cooler at the restaurant.

"I swear I can see that big eagle in there," he said to Delores as we stared at the diamond-like block of ice. "His eyes are fierce and his neck feathers are ruffled. All I have to do is chip away the leftover ice and he'll be there."

The night of the competition everyone was looking at Jason's ice sculptures instead of the food.

Jason's dad was standing by the crossed baseball bats that were surrounded by a baseball cap and three baseballs. "My son carved those."

"You must be very proud," a woman said.

"I am," Mr. Twelve Trees said.

And he hadn't even seen the centerpiece yet. Surrounded by roast turkeys, glazed hams, and jellied salads that looked like kaleidoscopes, was Jason's biggest ice carving, done especially for Delores. It was a baseball player, ball in hand, arm poised to throw, toe pointed like a ballet dancer, planted in the middle of an icy white base.

Jason understands the way Delores races around the bases, placing a foot solidly as she passes, staking out territory, making a statement, leaving her mark on each base.

Turbulence

I'm what's known as a white-knuckle flyer, even though some whiney Indians would say I was downplaying my Indianness by claiming to have white knuckles. Those are the same Indians who think just because they're Indians they should get published, no matter how bad a storyteller they are.

Anyway, my belly growls in fright when the landing gear is lowered on an approach, and when the plane revs up to race down the runway my lungs seems to rise right up and fill my mouth.

My friend Frank Fencepost try not to show it, but he's as uncomfortable in an airplane as I am. The way Frank put it is: "I ain't afraid of flying, I'm afraid of crashing."

Until this past school year I ain't had all that much experience at flying: a trip to England on a really huge plane that have a walk-around cocktail lounge, where Frank Fencepost spend his time touching the girl flight attendants; a flight to Las Vegas on a charter plane full of praying Lutherans; and a plane to the Arctic, where I end up out on the tundra inside a dead cariboo.

But since September I been flying once a week, on Tuesday nights, from Wetaskiwin to Grande Prairie, way up north of Edmonton. I go with a writer named Thomas Hanging Crow, who is a college teacher here in Wetaskiwin. Because I had some of my stories published in books he arrange for me to team-teach fiction writing for Native peoples.

"Teaching is how most writers put food on the table," Thomas say to me as we filling out about a thousand forms so there will be government money to pay me.

I don't understand why Native peoples should have a writing class all their own, and with Native teachers, too. To me it imply that Native people either ain't good enough to mix in with the white students, or else they're too good to mix with them. Either way is a losing situation. Story writing is story writing no matter the color of your skin.

I sure don't mind getting my pay for teaching, more than I make from the books I had published. That big, red roll of fifties make up for getting my pants scared off at least twice every flight.

Late every Tuesday afternoon we take off from Wetaskiwin Airport, which consist of one runway with some poles holding red-and-white socks that show what direction the wind is blowing. The little plane, which have the Alberta government crest on the door, look like it been made of old salmon tins flattened out and glued together. It have only one engine, like a car, and a pilot named Malloy trussed up like a turkey in front of a boardfull of flashing lights.

To get in the plane we have to bend up almost double. The

plane wiggle and jiggle and rattle like it going to for sure fall apart, before it even take off.

I'm always busy imagining us way up in the air, then plunging straight down when the engine quits. I see Ma and Sadie and Delores and Joseph and Illianna, even my white brother-in-law Bob McVey, standing around my grave, while a priest, who I sure didn't invite, say something nice about me.

About that point, after every take-off, the plane level off, and Thomas Hanging Crow touch me on the arm. "You can relax now, Silas. We got well over an hour before we land."

I let go of the armrests and relax my legs, which are braced against the seat in front of me. Sometimes I can actually feel my bones pop because I been holding them so tense.

"How come you don't get scared?" I ask Thomas Hanging Crow. He is too big for a little airplane like this, six-foot-four, 260 pounds or so. He have shiny black hair above an oblong face, black eyes, white teeth. He wear jeans, a cowhide vest, and cowboy boots and carries his black cowboy hat.

"It's simple," Thomas say. "I don't have a fear of dying."

"I'm not just saying this to make myself look good," I say after I've thought for a while, "but I don't think dying would be so bad. What I don't want is leave all my friends and family. I have things to do yet."

Now it is Thomas' turn to be silent for a while.

Never one to let a good silence last, I keep explaining.

"I want to get married to Sadie. I want us to have kids. I want to watch my sister's kids grow up. I want to be there to take care of Joseph, my retarded brother, and to see Ma don't want for nothing. I want to learn everything that Etta got to teach me about medicine and live long enough to maybe help a few people the way Etta done for the last sixty or seventy years."

"You're lucky," says Thomas Hanging Crow. "I used to have things to live for, too."

Thomas is fifty-five, though he don't have a single gray hair I can see, and the only sign of age is nice crinkly lines at the corners of his eyes. There are men of fifty on the reserve who look and act seventy. Thomas sure ain't one of those, so I'm surprised.

"I feel the same way about death you do," he says. "Death, in most instances, is not fearsome. But on every plane ride whenever we take off or land or run into turbulence, or on the road when something dangerous happens, I just think, 'I've done pretty well everything I wanted to do. If it's my time, I'm ready to go.' Saves a lot of stress and worry."

The plane made a lurch like one wing about to fall off. I grab the seat arms and stiffen my back, while Thomas act like he don't even notice.

"Turbulence doesn't bother me," Thomas goes on. He reach over and pry my hand off the chair arm. "When the plane goes into a dance like that I just think, 'I'm ready.' And, hey, I'm still here. And so are you. What good has your worrying done?"

Thomas been teaching at the community college in Wetaskiwin for about five years. Before that he was at a college in Manitoba.

His father was an Athabasca Indian from way up north somewhere. That was where Thomas was raised up, so far north the Indians are mostly Eskimos. His father marry a white woman come to teach at their reserve school; they have a couple of kids before he take off. Thomas' mom is dead, his sister live in New York City, married a Jewish man and Thomas ain't heard from her in years. He was married himself, with a daughter raised by her mother and step-father in Manitoba. I seen him posting a birthday parcel once, but I don't think he sees her.

He done awfully good at the university in Manitoba where he got his degrees; he published some stories early on, and a book I tried to read. It was about a writer named Thomas Wolfe, a white man in spite of his name, from North Carolina in the United States, who Thomas describe as a "garrulous bastard."

I had to look up *garrulous*.

As if he been reading my mind, Thomas say, "My daughter teaches Spanish in a Toronto high school. She lives with a boy I've never met. They want to have a hundred thousand dollars in the bank before they have children. I hope they get it saved up soon."

The plane lurch again and my stomach somersault. Turbulence ain't half as bad in a big plane, 'though it's scary, but I like the idea of four engines, 'cause I know one or even two can shut down without the plane crashing. But when there's only one engine . . . I mean, think how many times you stall your car at an intersection. In a small plane I imagine us dropping out of the sky like a shot duck. Splat!

We fly into Grande Prairie where a taxi meet us at the airport and drive us to the college, which is a bunch of concrete bunkers, where we hold a three-hour workshop for a group of Native writers. We start with fifteen students, but are down to eight, and probably only three or four will finish. But that's not bad. Most people ain't supposed to be writers though everybody think they can write a book. Thomas tell a story about a doctor who come up to a writer at a book-signing and say, "You know, when I retire I'm going to write a novel." And the author say back, "That's interesting, because when I retire I'm planning to do some brain surgery."

A couple of months ago Thomas Hanging Crow met Juanita Thompson. She just show up one class with a folder full of handwritten pages and ask if somebody would have a look at it. I offer to do it but she say no, she would rather have "that guy." I can tell from the look on her face it ain't really writing she got on her mind.

"I seen her around the school last year, and she say hello a couple of times in the cafeteria, but that's it," Thomas say as we taxiing back to the airport.

"She's kind of pretty," I say.

I'm guessing she's thirty-five, managed not to go to fat. She just fill out her jeans in all the right places, wear a red cardigan sweater with long sleeves that she push up to her elbows. Her complexion is clear and her eyes wide-spaced and the color of oak. Her hair come down past the middle of her back, and is parted so the left side of her face and her left eye is covered at least part of the time.

Thomas ignore me.

"She's not that good a writer. That folder had some emotional poetry in it, and a couple of autobiographical pieces, just a recital of all the bad things that have happened to her. They aren't really stories, but I can't seem to make her understand that."

"She's kind of pretty," I say again.

"Everybody have bad experiences to catalog. Real writers are the ones who change them into a story. Juanita don't understand that alcoholic parents, a sad childhood, boozy boyfriends, and a mean husband or two don't necessarily make for interesting reading. Like you told the class last week, Silas, 'Stories are not about events, but the people that events happen to.'"

The next week Juanita show up just as the class break for intermission, go right up to Thomas and start talking, then lead him off down the hall toward the cafeteria. The intermission last about ten minutes longer than usual, and eventually I start the class without Thomas.

On the plane ride back I keep bringing up Juanita and Thomas keep stonewalling me, until Thomas finally say, "I'm gonna let her sit in on the class, okay? She's not registered or anything, so this is just between us, right?"

"Right," I say.

It is only a couple more weeks until I am doing most of the second half of the class by myself. Then Thomas and Juanita go to the cafeteria after class while I cool my heels by the Coke machine in the hall, and Malloy get paid overtime because we're an hour late to the airport. Bet they'd have coffee before class too, if Thomas could schedule the flight earlier.

Then I hear that Thomas Hanging Crow drove all the way to Grande Prairie of a Friday night and don't get back until noon on Monday.

The week after that I walk into the Gold Nugget Café in Wetaskiwin and there is Thomas and Juanita sit side by side in a booth study the *Wetaskiwin Times*, the apartments for rent section.

"Juanita is coming to live in Wetaskiwin," Thomas says, noncommittally.

"We're looking for a bigger apartment," Juanita say, smile sideways at Thomas so pretty it make my mouth water to see how much in love she is.

"There's an opening in the mail room at the college here,"

Thomas say. "I arranged for Juanita to get the job. Beats hell out of her waiting tables in Grande Prairie."

"Now instead of only being together Tuesday nights, we're only apart Tuesday nights," Juanita say.

The week before Juanita move to Wetaskiwin, the assignment we give our class is to write a poem pretending they are something other than human, like a biscuit, barn door, or a bird in a cage.

Thomas is real proud of what Juanita turn in.

TURBULENCE
My life's been an airplane flight
No smooth journey
All takeoffs and landings
Turbulence, crosswinds, air pockets
The cabin too hot
The food cool and greasy

I find out later that Juanita have a son just graduate high school and gone to work for the paper mill in Grande Prairie, and a daughter already married, gonna produce a grandbaby in a couple of months.

"You determined to be a granddad one way or another," I say to Thomas during our Tuesday flight. Before he can answer the plane hit some bad air and we tip up like we flying sideways.

"Damn this rough air," say Thomas. "Hey, Malloy!" he yell toward the pilot. "How long you figure we got left to live?"

"Don't tell me you care about whether you live or die?" I say.

"Not me. I'm ready to go any time. I just hate being uncomfortable."

This afternoon I sure wish we didn't have to fly to Grande Prairie. It's the last class before Christmas break. I'd like to stay right at home in front of the fire, with Delores and Joseph getting all excited about Christmas, watch the leaf-sized snowflakes cover everything, and the chickadees bounce in the mountain ash tree behind the cabin.

It seem the gray sky get lower every moment and there is an evil crosswind blowing so hard the snow ticks like sand against the door of Louis Coyote's pick-up truck. I park it as out of the wind as I can, so at least the truck won't get drifted in.

From inside the airport hangar I see our plane warming up on the tarmac, the wind actually make the wings vibrate, like the plane was a dead dragonfly. A guy in gray coveralls and a wool hat is spraying something on the wings to keep them from icing up.

Juanita drop off Thomas Hanging Crow, her old red Oldsmobile with the one black fender clunking up to the door of the hangar. She slide from under the steering wheel and kiss Thomas long and serious. As he is pulling his briefcase out of the back seat, Juanita run around the car, her feet skidding on the snow, throw her arms around Thomas' neck and press her belly up against his. He kiss her back and wrap his big arms around her, lift her right off her feet while snowflakes collect in her long black hair like it turning white with age.

Thomas shake himself like a bear as he walk into the hangar.

"You sure we ought to do this?" I ask. "Weather ain't supposed to get no better."

"It's up to Malloy," says Thomas. "If he say go, we go."

Unfortunately, Malloy say go.

"Piece of cake," he says. "I flew in the Arctic for years. This is a summer day in the Arctic." He slap me on the shoulder, which don't make me feel any better.

The three of us climb the little toy steps into the cold interior of the plane. Thomas and I strap ourselves in. If I stretch my neck I can see Malloy check his instruments, squint more than I figure a pilot should. Snow cover most of the windshield, each side being only the area of a good-sized book to start with.

Thomas got his face buried in a novel, the way he always does, both hands on his book to keep the vibration from knocking it out of his hands.

We slither down the runway, me gripping the chair arms like I'd hold on to a tree if I was being swept down a river. The wheels beneath us finally stop bucking as we lift into the air. The plane is like a cork bobbing in water, bounce first one way, then another, groaning at its seams. I can see my breath in front of my face. My insides got cold knots in them.

Thomas Hanging Crow has closed his book, stuffed it between him and the window. He's sitting forward, gripping the arms of his chair, and I think I hear him whisper, "Juanita."

Saskatoon Search

"Hey, if you think you got nerve," says our new friend Baptiste Johnny, "my cousin Lenny over there never even flinched when he got bit by a badger supposed to be rabid."

Baptiste Johnny point to a dude sit about four tables away, have a red handkerchief tied around his neck is the only way we can tell him apart from maybe forty other guys in this huge bar in Williams Lake, or as Baptiste Johnny calls it, Willie's Puddle; a bar so big that my friend Frank Fencepost joke they should hire a tractor trailer to deliver beer to the tables.

"Lenny's hand was all gashed and the doctor was sewing him up, telling him that unless we could find that badger quick and get it tested, Lenny he'd have to take shots with this needle look like a six-inch spike that get rammed right into the middle of his belly every day for two weeks."

Across the room Lenny, who have a wicked little mustache like black silk straggling down over his lips, smile across the table at a real pretty girl in a buckskin jacket. He look a lot like a Brahma bull, hefty, built close to the ground, and mean.

"'So I might be rabid, eh?' Lenny say to the doctor.

"'That's right,' says the doc.

"'Better get me a pencil and paper then.'

"'You want to make a will?' ask the doctor.

"'No,' say Lenny, never bat an eye. 'I'm gonna make me a list of people I want to bite.'"

From across the bar, Lenny nod to Baptiste, but give me and Frank at least half an evil eye.

The trouble start almost as soon as we pick up the hitchhiker. He was standing on the edge of the road in the spitting rain, looking like a muskrat just stick his head up out of a lake. Me and Frank Fencepost are driving Louis Coyote's pick-up truck up a highway in the middle of British Columbia. On our way back from Vancouver we take the long way home, drive north to Dawson Creek, then south to Edmonton.

It wasn't us who decide this. Mad Etta, our medicine lady, covered over with a tarpaulin, sitting up in her tree-trunk chair in the box of the pick-up truck, say she heard a rumor that there was a place up in the middle of British Columbia where they grow the largest saskatoon berries in the world.

A four-hundred-pound medicine lady who once turned an RCMP constable into a weasel, make him stay that way for over a month, she usually get her way.

"You guys look like Indians, but not much," the hitchhiker say, as soon as he get himself comfortable, light up a cigarette.

"Guess we could say the same about you," say Frank. The stranger is short and barrel-chested, got his long hair in braids. He is all covered in denim and wearing construction boots, except when he unsnap his jean jacket we can see he wears a pair of rainbow-colored Police suspenders.

"This here outfit's called a Chilcotin tuxedo, partner," the strange Indian say, and he make the point by poking a stubby finger at Frank's chest.

"Be careful," warn Frank. "Last guy who pointed a finger at me ended up limping through the Yellow Pages."

The stranger have a good laugh at Frank's joke, explain that he is called Baptiste Johnny and is heading for a place called Williams Lake.

"What is this here Chilcotin you been talkin' about?" ask Frank. "Two or three towns we pass through I seen signs, Chilcotin this and Chilcotin that."

"It's a state of mind," say Baptiste Johnny.

"I like your suspenders there, partner," says Frank. "You know what they call a guy from our home town who wears a three-piece suit?"

"The defendant," say Baptiste Johnny, sure spoil hell out of Frank's joke, but it good to see we got things in common with people who live in the state of mind called Chilcotin.

Just then the load in the back shift, almost cause us to go in the ditch.

"What kind of cargo you haulin' back there?" ask Baptiste Johnny. "I seen your rear end was almost dragging on the blacktop."

"Live cargo," says Frank.

"Yeah? You either got a black bear or fifteen people back there."

"Etta can be anything she makes up her mind to be," says Frank.

First thing Etta ask Baptiste Johnny, right after we thrown back the tarp and Baptiste Johnny got over his surprise at Etta's size, was, "You know whereabouts the big saskatoons are?"

"I heard of them," say Baptiste Johnny, "supposed to be out in the bush from Williams Lake aways. But only medicine men know exactly where. Maybe they don't exist at all, likely some medicine man just dreamed them up to make himself look important."

"Maybe you better introduce me to your medicine man," says Etta.

I was kind of surprised to find out that the reason Etta searching for the giant saskatoons is purely personal. Two years in a row, at the Red Pheasant Sun Dance and Pow-Wow in Saskatchewan, Etta come second in the bannock-making contest. Etta don't like to be second to nobody. Bannock is flour and lard and saskatoon berries all mixed together, pounded, and dried to the texture of an old cow chip. Etta figure if she finds the giant saskatoon berries, she'll finally beat out that Saskatchewan medicine man named Ewalt Kicking-down-the-door.

"Them saskatoons supposed to be as big as golf balls," says Etta. "You slice 'em up like tomatoes. And sweet as young love. With them in my bannock it will win the blue-ribbon prize just like I bewitched the judges."

"Here I thought you wanted them to cure rheumatism or stomach trouble or something," I said.

"First things first," says Etta. "A medicine woman who lose a bannock-making contest also lose face."

"She could stand to lose about fifty pounds off that face," whisper Baptiste Johnny.

Soon as we hit town, Etta make a few inquiries, send off a few messages, arrange for a meeting with a local medicine man.

Back at the hotel in Williams Lake, Frank ask Baptiste Johnny why don't he invite his cousin Lenny *and* that real pretty girl in the buckskin jacket to join us for a beer?

"Well, I don't know," say Baptiste. "Lenny only goes where he wants to go."

"Hey," says Frank. "My uncle Zeke Fencepost was like that, a real loner. The only people come to his funeral was three inflatable women in black veils."

"Now Cousin Lenny might like to hear about *him*." Baptiste Johnny stand up and beckon Lenny and his pretty friend to come to our table.

Lenny shake my hand, hardly glance twice at me, but soon as he look at Frank he recognize trouble.

"Up here in the Chilcotin they call me the Town Tamer, eh?" he say directly to Frank. "I'm so tough the Hell's Angels ask my permission to come to this part of the country."

Frank ain't about to be outdone. "I can't get a good fight in Alberta no more, so I come up here to the Chilcotin where I heard you flat-faced Indians really know how to get rowdy."

"I'm so tough," counters Lenny, "that I wear my clothes out from the inside out."

But Frank can top even that. "I'm so tough," he says, "that on Hallowe'en, instead of bobbing for apples, I go down to the Gold Nugget Café and bob for french fries."

"What is this, the Canadian Legion Liars' Contest?" says Baptiste.

Next morning, Lenny he say to us, "You guys want to go for a ride?"

"Where to?" we say.

"Don't matter. Nothin' like an after-breakfast drive in a big, new car to start the day right."

"We gonna steal one?" ask Frank.

"Hey, partner, we never steal. We borrow," says Lenny. "We'll just watch the door of this hotel for a few minutes. I'll let you know when the perfect one comes along."

"That's the one," he say, about ten minutes later, as a big, new Buick stop in the circular driveway and a well-dressed white lady get out. "Keys in the car," say Lenny, hopping up and down. "Probably a full tank of gas. Let's go."

"But there's kids in the car," says Frank. "No way we can steal kids."

"That's what that lady is counting on," says Lenny.

We walk around the car, peer in the windows, admire the deep velvet seats. There is a boy about five in the front, a baby in a car seat in the back.

Lenny tap on the side window, smile real nice at the kid who push a button and the power window whirr down.

"Your mom want you to bring the baby inside," Lenny say. "We'll give you a hand to get her out of the car seat, okay?"

The little kid open up the door. We release the kid's seat belt while Lenny untangle the baby from the car seat and fit her into the little boy's arms. He even shield the baby's face from the wind with the corner of the pink blanket.

"Wouldn't want her to catch cold, would we?" he say to the kid, who smile because he is real proud to be helping his mother. "Just wait by the front desk for your mama," Lenny say. He pat the kid on the head, send him up to the hotel door.

"Okay, let's roll," say Lenny, as at least ten of us climb over each other getting into the Buick.

Lenny get behind the wheel. He burn rubber for at least a block, and we doing eighty miles an hour by the edge of town.

A mile or so down the highway he turn onto a country road, which pretty soon deteriorate to a dirt road, then to a trail, then to nothing at all. But Lenny drive just as if we was still on blacktop.

"When Cousin Lenny there was in Boy Scouts," say a guy we ain't seen before, "only knot he learned was the noose."

We rip off the muffler and whatever ever else can get torn off the bottom of a car by rocks and logs, also do the passenger side a certain amount of damage get too close to a big tree.

I say, "When my friend Frank there was born, the doctor told his mother, 'Water it twice a week and keep it out of bright sunlight.'"

"That's enough from you, Standing-neck-deep-in-muddy-water," Frank say, after he come up from kissing on that girl in the buckskin jacket. Him and that girl get along like a couple of bandits.

"I think," the girl say to Frank, "I get you adopted into the Carrier Tribe. Once that's done you never be able to go away from the Chilcotin."

"Not necessary," say Frank. "One time I went to a doctor in Edmonton and he told me straight out I was a carrier."

After we arrive in Williams Lake, but before we went to the bar, Baptiste took Frank and me to his cousin's house where he arrange for all three of us to spend the night. It is kind of like at home in Hobbema, everybody with Indian blood is a cousin of some kind, and Janet Ghostkeeper at least trust Baptiste Johnny well enough to let him bring strangers into her house. The pretty girl Lenny was with just up and disappear late in the evening. I sleep on a blanket behind the sofa, but as far as I can tell, Frank never turn up at all. Last I seen of him he was going to meet a blonde girl who wait tables at the Last Chance Café, supposed to get off work at 4:00 a.m.

Me and Baptiste and Lenny head to the Last Chance for breakfast, meet Frank coming down the street, grin like a pumpkin.

"Were you tipi-crawling?" says Lenny.

"No tipis for me," says Frank. "Went home to a nice warm apartment with that girl from the Last Chance."

"Not the blonde?" says Lenny.

"The blonde," says Frank.

He look glum. "Me and Baptiste been hustling her for two years, all we ever got from her were dirty looks."

"What can I say?" says Frank. "She just never come up against a Fencepost before."

"Was she good?" ask Baptiste.

"That woman's so hot she could cook meat with her bare hands. Only trouble is, she was so white I kept losing her in the sheets."

Most of the day we riding all around the backwoods of the Chilcotin. Ain't a lot left of the Buick by the time Lenny abandon it, and we hitch a ride back to Willie's Puddle with a guy named Moses in a pick-up truck even more beat-up than Louis Coyote's.

"Ain't you afraid the RCMP gonna pounce on us soon as we hit town?" I ask.

"Hey," says Lenny. "What kind of description you figure the RCMP got of the car thieves, eh? Heavy-set Native males with long hair, some braided some not, some with mustaches, some not, all wearing jean jackets. Fit 90 percent of the men in the Chilcotin."

While we been getting rowdy, Etta been doing some detective work. She gone through a couple of medicine men who don't know nothing. But a third one tell her if she's a real medicine woman she be able to smell out the giant saskatoons all by herself, not need any help.

"I like his style," says Etta. "Fire up the truck."

It is dark by the time we get Etta loaded up, and it seem like we got every Indian in the Chilcotin traveling with us. Just as we pulling out of town, the truck and us making a certain amount of racket, an RCMP car pull in behind us, lights flashing.

Frank start to pull over.

"Make a run for it!" yell everybody. "It's Constable Mooseface."

"What the point?" says Frank. "He got our license number."

"Your license plates are under the seat. Me and Lenny took care of that," says Baptiste Johnny. "We're just another beat-to-ratshit pick-up truck full of Indians. Now boot it, partner."

Baptiste direct Frank onto a logging road crookeder than Chief Tom Crow-eye and Samantha Yellowknees put together.

"Fencepost will show you how to outrun a mountie," says Frank.

"In this truck?" say Lenny. "You couldn't drive out of sight in two days."

"One time," I say, "somebody with a speedometer timed this here truck on a straightaway in Alberta. Foot-to-the-floor Frank Fencepost there got it the all way up to forty-eight miles an hour."

"My skill at evasive driving make up for my lack of speed," say Frank.

On one of the sharp curves the truck tip about three-quarters of the way over, then right itself all of a sudden, spurt ahead like a kernel of corn just been popped. I think I hear some commotion in the back. Even though our lights are off and it pouring rain, the RCMP car stick to our tail just like we was towing him.

"About a mile further on there's a fork in the road," say Baptiste. "Keep left until the last second then take the right fork."

That fork is on us before we know it. Frank swing right at the last second, almost tip us over again. The RCMP keep left and disappear.

"You can slow down now," says Baptiste.

"We built that left fork with a borrowed bulldozer a few days ago," say Lenny, "just for a night like this. That fork only runs thirty yards then there's a nice deep slough. Constable Mooseface will be wet to the gonads by the time he wades out."

Another ten miles or so the road disappear altogether, and we drive cross-country for a while. Baptiste tell Frank to stop in front of a cabin appear in a clearing, have a coal oil lamp burn in its window.

"My cousin, Barbara Johnny," says Lenny.

"My cousin, too," says Baptiste. "And she make the best dandelion wine in all the Chilcotin."

"Anybody live around here ain't your cousin?" ask Frank.

"Constable Mooseface," says Baptiste.

"How come you call him Constable Mooseface?" we ask Baptiste Johnny.

"When that constable first come here," he answer, "somebody offer to teach him Indian. He think he's learning to say 'How can

I help you?' but he is actually saying 'I am Constable Mooseface. Let's get naked.'"

Frank tell Baptiste Johnny how, every summer, when the local priest, Father Alphonse, go on holidays, the church send in a replacement.

"First thing we do with that new priest is tell him the way to impress his congregation is to learn a few phrases of Cree. Then, so he won't be suspicious, we take him to Blind Louis Coyote. Louis is way over eighty, wear buckskins, have long white hair and milk-colored eyes. Louis speak soft and act gentle as rainwater. The visiting priest never suspect a thing.

"At Sunday mass, what show up is over a hundred people, cram the pews to bursting, to hear the priest give his welcome speech what Louis Coyote been rehearsing with him all week.

"The priest stand up real serious and recite the words Louis have him memorize. He begin by saying, 'Hide your daughters! I am Muskrat Breath.' Then he tell how naked he is under his black robe, and how he done things with his mother would land just about anybody in jail. Everybody smile and nod, clap their hands when he finish, just as if he on 'The Tonight Show.'

"After mass he shake our hands, repeat to each of us, 'Hide your daughters! I am Muskrat Breath,' which he think is some kind of greeting, while we smile and smile. Bet he wonders why there is only seven or eight old ladies in babushkas at church next week."

When we get out of the truck, the tarpaulin and the tree-trunk chair is still there, but Mad Etta ain't nowhere to be found.

"Remember when we went around that corner on a wheel and a half?" say Frank, "And how the truck suddenly went faster?"

"Four hundred pounds lighter," I say.

There are several scared-looking people in the truck box. "Yonder big lady topple off her chair, roll right over the tailgate," they say.

"Etta is sure gonna be cross," says Frank.

"And wet."

"And bruised."

"The longer we leave her out there the worse it gonna be," I say. "We better start back."

"What do you mean start back?" say Lenny. "Parties here in the Chilcotin usually go on for four or five days, and we ain't even got started yet."

We go inside Barbara Johnny's cabin, have us a quick glass of dandelion wine, listen to a few Merle Haggard records on her wind-up record player, spend only a hour, well, not more than two, anyway, then we head back to look for Etta.

On the way we catch up with Constable Mooseface hiking along the trail, a weak little flashlight glinting on the puddles.

Frank pull the truck over.

"Well, who have we got here?" says Constable Mooseface, peer in the window of the truck.

"We just a bunch of law-abiding citizens out for an evening drive. We don't usually pick up strangers," say Frank. "Never know what kind of riffraff you find on a dark road in the middle of the night. But you got an honest face, officer, so climb right in."

Etta is right where we left her, landed on her back in the muddy ditch, kind of like a beetle, not able to kick herself over on her stomach.

She is some upset with us, call us names I didn't even know she knew. But once we get her upright, instead of doing us all serious physical harm, even though Etta is wet as a drowned bear, mean-looking as a sasquatch, she is smiling.

Etta slam off through the undergrowth, travel about a mile, maybe more, with everyone, including Constable Mooseface, following along.

"Silas! Smell the air!" she say to me.

I smell the air. Smell like regular bush country to me.

"Stay put!" she tells everybody and crashes off again. The sounds of Etta in the underbrush seem to come from all directions at once.

"Bad medicine, bad medicine," Lenny the Town Tamer keep repeating. I wouldn't have thought of him as being a believer in the old ways. I thought he was just mad at Frank for messing with his girlfriend.

When Etta finally come back, from a different direction than she went away, she carrying her babushka like a pail, and inside, 'though at first I think they are wild plums, are about fifty giant saskatoons. In the truck box on the way back she let me eat one, and even though regular saskatoons are the best-tasting berries in the world, this giant saskatoon is so sweet and taste so *purple*, I know my mouth gonna water for years every time I think about it.

Next morning, when we ready to leave town, Frank he's sent both his white and Indian girlfriends on errands so he be a good twenty-five miles up the road toward Dawson Creek before they discover Frank spent half the night with each of them. "Hey," Frank explain, "I'm an equal opportunity stud," but Baptiste Johnny point out that Lenny hanging around down the block looking mean as a hail storm.

"You shouldn't have messed with Lenny's woman," somebody say. "Lenny didn't exactly turn you in to the RCMP, but he let them know when they questioning him about the borrowed Buick that you Alberta Indians are probably responsible for most of the crimes around here."

"A Fencepost knows no fear," says Frank. "Hey, a Fencepost has strands of steel wire for blood, an anvil in each fist . . . "

As me and Frank walk around the corner to where our truck parked, we see Etta and her giant saskatoons about to climb in the truck when Lenny come running down the sidewalk like he's being chased by something with sharp teeth carrying a shotgun.

He wrench the babushka from Etta's hand, say something about the secret of Chilcotin saskatoons not going back to Alberta, and race right on down the street.

When Lenny come by, Frank just stick out his foot and he take off through the air like a football player about to make a tackle, land hard, skid on his face for about twenty feet, and lay still. The giant saskatoons go bouncing like ping-pong balls, but not for all that far. Etta already waddling purposefully after them.

Frank smile and shake his head. "Real dangerous to run that fast. See what happens when a guy blows a moccasin at fifty miles an hour?"

When we're a good long ways down the road, Etta bang on the back window, and me and Frank both look at her, me pretty well keeping the truck on the road. Etta not only got her babushka of giant saskatoons, she's pulled from somewhere on her person, wrapped in wet newspapers, several slips from those saskatoon trees. Nice to know that next year when the Saskatchewan bannock-making contest come along we don't have to go on another saskatoon search in the Chilcotin.

"Look out!" yell Frank, as a semitrailer breathe past us, even though we were mostly in his lane.

The Rain Birds

"Lawyers," say my friend Frank Fencepost, "need a stack of paper high enough to burn a wet moose before they even take your case."

Me and Frank, Bedelia Coyote, and Mad Etta, our medicine lady, are sitting around the living room of Melvin Dodginghorse's big split-level farmhouse. Melvin been complaining that lawyers ain't been able to help with his problems.

At least until this summer, Melvin has been a real successful farmer.

"He have so much land, just looking at it make me tired," says Frank.

Among the many things that me and Frank Fencepost and my friends ain't is farmers.

Melvin and his family live like white people — two cars, a microwave oven, and a year ago he even set up his own computer.

"I'd sure like one of them computers," say Frank, who spend a lot of time since he learn to read and write messing with the computer at the Tech School in Wetaskiwin, where him and me take classes. "I'd get me a program called MacSperm, help me keep track of all the rug rats I've fathered. My motto is 'A Fencepost in every oven.'"

We haven't always been good friends of Melvin's, especially after we helped his daughter get together with a boyfriend Melvin didn't like. But things blow over, and Melvin even like his son-in-law now, and he especially like his granddaughter Buffalo Jump Woman (Buffy) who's just old enough to climb on his knee and hug his neck.

As we were driving over to Melvin's, Etta in the back of the pick-up on her tree-trunk chair, we joke that Melvin Dodging-horse musta used up all the options in the white world if he calling for superstition and Mad Etta.

Melvin's problem is his water supply is disappearing, being stole right from under his fields. Computer farmers have bought or leased all the land to the west and south of our reserve.

They put up expensive white-board fences where their land touch Highway 2A, and there is about five acres of lawn with flower beds full of sweet petunias, marigolds, and purple-and-white pansies that surround that computer building. There are two flagpoles at least fifty feet tall with Canadian and Alberta flags bigger than a bedsheet. There is a sign, low to the ground, four-foot-tall gold letters on a white background, spell out "Environment Farms of Canada."

"Even their name make it sound like they doing something good," say Mad Etta, but she frown when she say it.

That whole twenty-five thousand acres is managed by one cowboy in a plaid shirt and clean jeans, who don't even have a suntan. He sit all day in a concrete-block shack and stare at the bluey screen of a computer that tell him which acres need watering, fertilizing, weeding, or harvesting. When a job needs doing, he pick up a phone and, like magic, trucks full of workers appear to do the job the computer suggested.

"I bet you could be God if you wanted," Frank said, the time we visited that shack.

The pale cowboy didn't answer, but he smiled like he knew secrets we didn't.

The computer farmers grow crops that require more water than normal. Instead of wheat or oats or barley, they growing things like peas and cucumbers, plants that drink a lot.

To get enough water, they irrigate; "irritate," Frank call it. They drilled huge, deep wells and brought in wheel-line sprinklers, stand fifty feet tall, is built like the daddy-long-legs that dance over quiet slough water in summer.

Sometimes of a summer evening, when the weather is soft and the evening sky pink, me and my friends park on a country road far from the pale cowboy's concrete cabin, walk into the fields, and play like little kids in the cool water that drift down from the rain-birds.

Those wells suck up millions of gallons of water from underground streams, including streams under the reserve, particularly under Melvin's farm.

Not long after the computer farming corporation get established, a man wearing a western suit and a million-dollar smile come around the reserve and give a talk at Blue Quills Hall.

"We want to be good corporate neighbors," he say to us.

And we believe him.

"We will introduce several million dollars into the economy of central Alberta," the man went on. "Our studies show that we will put 30 percent more money into local hands than if each farm was individually owned and operated."

At first no one suspect what is happening. The computer farms was green and prosperous, load up the produce, and haul it off to Edmonton and Calgary.

Environment Farms been operating for almost three seasons when we first notice the bad taste. People who live along the south side of the reserve finding that their well water turn a pale yellow color, taste like a used car tire smell.

"Gopher piss," say Frank, spit a mouthful into Gus Cardinal's feed lot.

"The voice of an expert," I say to Gus.

"Cattle won't drink the stuff no more," Gus says. "I have to drive my herd two miles north, drink surface water from Jump-off-Joe Creek."

Melvin Dodginghorse take a water sample to the District Agriculturist in Wetaskiwin.

"Nitrates," is the answer he get back.

"Nitrates are seeping into the underground water supply," the District Agriculturist say. "They come from the computer farms. They use about five times as much commercial fertilizer as ordinary farmers, forcing the land to produce two crops in the short Alberta growing season."

Don't take Bedelia Coyote long to get her back up. She has friends who are greener than Kermit the Frog.

"Poison! Law suits! Birth defects!" cry Bedelia and her friends before they even have their first meeting.

"Speaking of birth defects," say Frank, "you hear about the 250 women on the reserve who was born without tits? The Indian-nippleless 500. Ha!"

If you ever been in the Parliament Building in Edmonton, first thing you notice is that every floor is circular. You can stand in the middle of the main floor, tip your head back and stare right up to the top of the dome.

"They do that so nobody can catch them on the corners," say Mad Etta, the time I drove her to see all the white marble and varnished wood in that stone building what smell of used paper and slow service.

The first thing Chief Tom Crow-eye, who is our MLA representative in Edmonton, say when we tell him what the problem is — "Environment Farms are our good corporate neighbors."

So we know how much help we'll get from the provincial government. And the only time the big government in Ottawa ever look at the west is if they figure they can steal something.

"Environment Farms may not know a lot about farming but they sure know their politics," say Bedelia Coyote. "They greased Chief Tom so good he don't have to drive to Edmonton; he just take a good run and slide the whole forty miles."

The pale cowboy say he will pass the complaint on to their Calgary office, and Calgary say it is something should be handled by the head office, in someplace that sound like *Mississippi*, Ontario. It is three months before they finally send a letter to us.

"Yes," they say, "your water does taste and smell bad, and you have our sympathy. However, after extensive investigation, there is no scientific evidence to show that your problem is related to our farming activities."

The problem, they tell us, is likely caused by natural sulfur deposits way below ground, the kind that make hot springs in some parts of the province.

"Dig deep wells," they say, and, as good corporate neighbors, offer us their well-drilling equipment at only half their normal rates.

The problems get worse. It is a dry summer. Environment farms irrigate more than ever. Some of the wells on the reserve stop producing altogether. Melvin Dodginghorse's crops lie brittle and dying in his fields.

"Environment Farms has pumped the water out from under your land," the District Agriculturist say sadly. "And coupled with the drought . . ." he shrug his shoulders.

Before we went to the meeting at Melvin's house we took a drive south of the reserve, stopped a couple of times on country roads where it was so silent the world might have already ended. At one spot I bet there wasn't a human being for twenty miles in any direction.

The computer farms have bulldozed farm houses and outbuildings, leveled the land, and planted it to crop. No matter how hard we try or how good our memories, we can't pick out a spot where a single set of buildings used to be.

"You're the medicine woman. Why don't you do something?" some of our people say to Mad Etta.

"A crooked stick will cast a crooked shadow," say Etta, look very pleased with herself.

"What's that got to do with anything?"

"Nature always win in the end," say Etta.

"Nature already been outfoxed, outnumbered, and outclassed."

Etta snort softly, like she do when someone from the government try to tell her they are there to help. Or like the time I suggest she should have the electricity installed so she could have a TV, and that maybe a microwave could cook up her medicines quicker than the woodstove.

Etta snort that snort and growl, "If I want the electricity, I'll make some myself."

Bet she could, too.

A couple of summers ago, Bedelia got stirring things up.

"That computer farm hires dozens, sometimes hundreds of part-time workers to harvest their crops," she say one afternoon at Hobbema Pool Hall, "and how many of them are Indian?"

"Six percent?" answer Frank, pick a number out of the air.

"Closer than you think," say Bedelia. "Do you know they truck people out from Wetaskiwin and even Edmonton? There are four thousand people on the reserve right here and 70 percent of them are unemployed."

"Indians ain't farmers," Frank answer, go on to quote Crowchild, Poundmaker, even Young Eagle — every famous Indian who had bad things to say about farming.

The argument go on all afternoon and evening, but Bedelia arrange that the next time Environment Farms put out a call for day workers, thirty or so of us be ready to answer.

Boy, if there's one thing I hate it is getting up early in the morning. The dew is thick on the grass and the sun just peeping over the horizon when that flatdeck truck pick us up at Hobbema General Store, carry us to the fields. They harvest the peas with a huge machine look like seven street sweepers joined together.

"Now that is what I call tearing up the pea patch," say Frank.

The foreman wear bib-overalls and a yellow straw hat, hand out baskets, assign us rows, and tell us what size of cucumbers to pick and what size to leave alone. Another couple of guys spend their time watching us. Guess they figure we might try to get even.

"Wait a minute," the foreman say when he spot Lawrence Canvas. Lawrence is over eighty years old, blind, have only one leg. "How can that guy pick cucumbers?"

"Lawrence is one of the few survivors of the battle of Little Big Mouth," say Frank.

"You mean Little Big Horn," correct the foreman.

"Little Big Mouth was my first wife," say Lawrence. "I outlived two more since her."

"Only one," say Mrs. Canvas. "Two dead altogether."

"I have known many cucumbers," say Lawrence. "I can harvest eggs from beneath a hen. Cucumbers do not run away, I simply find a vine and follow it along until there isn't any more vine."

"Well. . ."

"If you don't hire me I'll make it rain."

The foreman squint and stare at Lawrence for a few seconds before he thrust a basket into Lawrence's hands.

After people picked their cucumbers, the baskets was emptied into a wire-mesh cage big as a semitrailer and towed by a tractor. The cage full of cucumbers was then towed up to the Environment Farms warehouse where the cukes get put into real trucks and carried off to Edmonton.

The first time the cage was full of cucumbers the foreman ask for someone to drive the tractor over to the warehouse. I put up my hand to volunteer, but Frank was already firing up the engine without benefit of a key.

"'King of the road,' they call me," Frank tell the foreman. "Eighteen-wheeler is my middle name. Ten-four. Roger, Good

Buddy. Hammer down, the bears are in hiding," and Frank take off with a screech.

You probably seen on TV what happened next. We was picking cucumbers on the east side of Highway 2A, and the warehouse was on the west side. Frank got himself and the tractor across the highway, but the wire cage and about half a million cucumbers met up with an eighteen-wheeler full of steel rods.

"Instant fresh cucumber relish," is the way Frank describe it.

The cucumbers make such a squishy mess that cars driving along Highway 2A skid into each other or into the ditch. It take the RCMP over twelve hours to get everything back to normal, with Constable Chrétien and Constable Bobowski covered in cucumber slime.

Frank, of course, get fired, and over the next three days the rest of us quit, all except old Lawrence Canvas, who turn out to be their best picker.

"You figure you worked long enough to apply for unemployment?" somebody ask.

"No need," say Frank. "We're already unemployed."

It was Bedelia Coyote who, through her connections with every protest group carry a poster or raise a clenched fist, got a civil-rights lawyer name of Mr. Elmore to take Melvin Dodginghorse's case.

The day that the case finally get a hearing, Mr. Elmore, Melvin, and Bedelia sit at one table, while six large, gray-suited lawyers, look like they had the same parents, stare at their reflections at another.

"The judge has taken the case under advisement," Mr. Elmore tell us at the end of the day. "Translated, that means he doesn't have any idea how or what he should decide, so he'll think about it for a year or two, hope like hell the problem goes away before he has to make a decision."

"Should put Melvin, Mad Etta, and them corporate lawyers all in a sweat lodge for a few hours," say Frank. "Decisions are a lot easier when you're naked."

"You just have to be patient," Mr. Elmore went on, smiling in a slow, friendly way. "In spite of what it looks like, Environment Farms Corporation is losing money."

That bit of information start Bedelia poking around in financial statements.

"They have millions of dollars invested in irrigation equipment, tractors, trucks, harvesting equipment. They're in a financial corner," Bedelia say.

"But how can they not make money?" I asked.

"What they forgot," says Bedelia, "was the human factor. None of the men who make up the color brochures, graphs, and charts has ever farmed. They never got up at four in the morning to milk cows; never had shit on their shoes.

"They figure that if a farmer and his wife can farm 640 acres with limited financing and inefficient equipment, they can make big money by farming that 640 acres and 25,000 more without the farmer or his wife, just with scientific methods."

"So why doesn't it work?"

"They forgot farmers work twenty-hour days, because they love the land. They don't even earn minimum wage. Environment Farms have to pay three shifts a day. When we worked there we went home after eight hours — and only worked as hard as we had to."

When we tell all this to Etta, she look like she's known it all along.

The last while I notice Etta's been rumbling around the reserve late at night. I hear her talking down in the slough, making conversation with someone who may not be there. Every day for the past week there's been a late afternoon gully washer of a thunderstorm dump oceans of water on the reserve.

I think I hear Mad Etta snorting softly, saying "Nature always win in the end."

There is the story about Etta and the Northern Lights.

George the Cat

Cats are all the time pretending —
Bobbie Ann Mason

As I was hiking up the road toward her place, Rita Makes-room-for-them was ambling down the footpath from the door of her broken-down house, heading toward the gravel road and the lunch-bucket-shaped mail box. The black lettering that had long ago read "Rita & Sanderson Makes-room-for-them" was faded beyond recognition, and the pole that Sanderson had cut, hewn, and creosoted was wormy and pitched forward so that if the mail box had been human its chin would nearly have been touching the ground.

"I'm in about the same condition as that goddamn mail box," Rita said.

Rita is a big, thick woman a little over thirty, with wide-set brown eyes in a tobacco-colored face. Her hips are wide and her backside fills out her Levi's. She is wearing a blue work shirt and a wide black belt that I've seen Sanderson wear sometimes. My guess is Rita is an inch or two bigger around the waist.

"What you doin' here, Silas?"

"Sanderson was giving me a ride to Bluff Corners on his way home, but the truck hit a pothole, the front passenger tire blew, and we came out on the short end of a scuffle with a deep ditch full of water."

Rita shakes her head. She's spent her life receiving bad news.

"Sanderson okay?"

"Other than a bump on the head and being mad as a castrated goat."

"So how come you're here?"

"Well, Sanderson figured you'd worry if he was any later than he is already, so he sent me to tell you where he is."

"He was supposed to be home yesterday afternoon. If I didn't die of worry overnight another few hours wasn't going to hurt."

Rita bent way down and peeked into the mail box.

"What the hell?" she said, jumping back.

"What?"

"There's some animal in the goddamn mail box."

There was a piece of two-by-four lying in the ditch. "Hope it ain't a skunk," I said, reaching for it.

"I am certainly not a skunk," said a voice from the mail box. "Thanks for waking me up."

Rita scowled, placing her large right hand on her denim hip. I picked up the two-by-four and took a step toward the mail box. The door hung permanently open about three inches, but it was too dark to see exactly what was inside.

"Sanderson, is that you?" Rita asked. "You're playing a trick, right?"

"Tape recorder," I said.

Rita gingerly reached forward to pull open the door of the mail box. I stood to her left, the piece of two-by-four held like a baseball bat.

As Rita snapped the door fully open, a good-sized yellow cat poked his head slowly out of the mail box, looked both ways, and, as Rita jumped back and I flexed the two-by-four, leaped to the ground at our feet, landing awkwardly, front paws sort of collapsing.

"What the hell?" said Rita.

"Be careful with that stick. You could do me serious damage," the cat said to me.

"He talked," Rita said. "You talked," she said to the cat, who sat on his haunches, eyeing me balefully.

I reached carefully into the mail box. There was nothing but a couple of advertising flyers and some yellow cat hair. No tape recorder. No microphone.

"You talked," Rita said again, staring down. "But you're a . . ."

"Cat," said the cat. "George the Cat."

"Yeah, well every other goddamn thing is wrong in my life," said Rita. "No reason I shouldn't find a talking cat in my mail box."

The cat was as disreputable a cat as I'd ever seen. It was an average-sized, square-jawed yellow tom cat, but he looked as if he'd recently stuck a paw in a light socket and had probably slept for several nights in blackberry briars. He was scrawny, with uneven whiskers on each side of a scarred face. One eye watered and was half-closed in a permanent squint. His ears looked as if they'd been nibbled by hungry fish.

"I fell asleep while I was waiting for someone to show up," George the Cat said, speaking very clearly. In spite of looking like a cat wino, he spoke with an educated voice, sort of like my friend Mr. Nicholls down at the Tech School in Wetaskiwin.

"Sorry," he went on, "no personal mail, just a flyer from

K-Mart — no real bargains — and some advertising from Robinson's Stores — a good price on bicycle pumps, if you happen to need one."

"So, to what do I owe the pleasure of a talking cat?" asked Rita.

"You don't quite understand," said George the Cat, looking like something ejected from a garbage barrel, stretching to within a foot of Rita's scuffed black boots with the hand-tooled R on them. "I'm your power animal."

Rita guffawed. "You?"

"Why not?" George the Cat sounded vaguely offended.

"You're a cat."

"True."

"A mangy . . ." she kicked gravel and yellowish dust in George's direction, "goddamned barn cat who looks half dead. You've probably got ticks . . ."

"I admit to being down on my luck."

"Then don't even think about being my power animal. This is a joke, right? Gloria Lefthand set this up, right? Silas, you're in on it. That fucking Sanderson, there's been no accident. There's a tape recorder in the ditch . . ."

Rita stared out across the open prairie. There was nothing visible except the purplish hulk of Gloria Lefthand's house a mile cross country. She stared up the path toward her own house, a pitiful frame structure supplied by the Department of Indian Affairs about thirty years ago. It had once been painted a brilliant aquamarine. Somebody in Ottawa heard that Indians like bright colors, so the houses got painted rose and yellow, sky blue and crow-wing purple.

"No joke," said George the Cat.

"I should have known," said Rita. "Other people get a bear, a wolverine, an eagle. I get a barn cat looks as if it's got the distemper. I'm not a bad person, Silas. Why does this happen to me?"

"Never underestimate your generic barn cat," said George, moving out of range of Rita's boots, just in case.

"Yeah, well, all I need is another mouth to feed," said Rita. "And that's what you are, aren't you?"

George appeared to shrug.

"Sanderson's just out of jail, not that he didn't deserve to be there, and he's wrecked the truck. My car's sitting five miles down the pike with the tranny locked tighter than a banker's fist. It's been there for a week so kids have probably stripped it down until it looks like it's been X-rayed. I'm overdrawn at the Credit Union, and my kid needs an eye operation or she's gonna grow up to look like you.

"The welfare check's late. My twelve-year-old looks sixteen and is threatening to run off with a twenty-year-old named Billy Kills-his-own-horses, who has a record a mile long and whose only ability seems to be breaking his bones at rodeos and taking part in the closing-time riot at the Alice Hotel Bar. You want to hear about my big troubles?"

"One of my good qualities is that I'm an excellent listener," said George the Cat.

"I'm outa cigarettes," said Rita. "You wouldn't happen to have . . . ?" She stopped herself.

George's voice had a whiskey-soaked edge to it. He reminded me of an old, red-haired cowboy I met in a bar in Ponoka one time.

"Nobody ever said life was fair," said George the Cat.

"Thanks. You're a regular Phil Donahue. Instead of a screaming hawk I get a philosopher with fleas."

I took out my cigarettes and offered Rita one. She lit up and inhaled deeply.

"Things are getting better already," said George.

"So, what are you gonna do for me, power animal?"

"Perhaps if we strolled up to your house, you might have a saucer of milk to spare? I suppose a bit of cat food would be too much to hope for?"

"You'd be right. Catch yourself a field mouse, great hunter."

"Don't worry about me. I'm a cat, and cats suffer."

"A theologian, too?"

"I'm also a survivor. There was an emperor in Egypt who sent out an order to kill all the cats."

"So the Jews had Hitler, the Indians had the white man. You're not the only one who's been persecuted," said Rita.

"May I point out that Indians have reserves, the Jews have Israel. When you consult an atlas do you see any place called Catland?"

"What am I supposed to do, lead a hundred thousand cats to seize North Dakota?"

"I also have an excellent sense of humor. Those who are persecuted survive by making fun of their persecutors."

Rita laughed out loud.

"Jesus, Silas, do you believe this. I'm having a real conversation with a goddamn cat. So," Rita said to George, "What do you think of Morris?"

George's tail twitched.

"He has a certain panache," said George. "But he wouldn't last on the street for ten minutes. Now I don't have any proof of this, a rumor only, but it wouldn't surprise me if he was gay."

"Hey, one thing I've always wanted to know . . . how do you purr?"

"Can you explain the intricate operation of your digestive system?"

"No."

"Cats purr, that's all."

"Okay, so tell me something interesting about cats. Something that most people don't know."

"Let me see," said George.

We were walking, the three of us, up the path toward Rita's house. We both offered to carry George, but he declined.

"Do I look that bad?"

"You do," I said.

"Let me see," George repeated. "Are you aware that cats have twelve-hour orgasms?"

Rita laughed out loud.

"Did you know that a cat dressed as a baby survived the sinking of the *Titanic?*"

George's tail is straight up like a flagpole.

"Did you know that a cat rode to Little Big Horn in General Custer's saddlebag?"

"Do you know what Custer was wearing at his last stand?" I say. "An Arrow shirt. Ha!"

"Boo," says George the Cat.

"I mean, you gotta be kidding," says Rita, "you can't possibly be my power animal."

"I can talk. Doesn't that impress you? You do believe in power animals, don't you?"

"Good question," says Rita. "Silas, what do you think? Do we believe in power animals?"

Mad Etta, our medicine lady, has made some genuine magic a couple of times in my life. I know all the stories about power animals, but I've never had any experience.

"I guess it depends," I say.

"Great. Nothing like a definitive stand. If this thing we're talking to ain't a power animal, what do you suppose it is?"

"When you climbed out of the mail box, you said you were waiting for someone. Who were you waiting for?" I ask.

"I was waiting for someone to come walking down that road. I thought it might have been you, but I was wrong."

"So, who are you waiting for?" asks Rita.

"I guess I'll know when they get here."

"I think you're just a mooch. You're probably a reincarnation of my uncle."

In an hour or two, George the cat drank up two cups of milk, ate a cold cooked pork chop, a slice of mock chicken luncheon meat, and a plate of Kraft Dinner, which Rita made for her and me for lunch.

"You know what would solve a lot of the problems of the world?" asks George.

"If I was to win about fifteen million bucks in the lottery?" says Rita.

"If everyone learned to speak Cat, instead of having all these multiple dialects and languages."

"There's just one cat language?" says Rita.

"You can bring a cat off the boat from China or Sweden, one who's never heard a word of English, and we'll communicate like we've been buddies all our lives. By the way, did you know I have an IQ of 131? The Kuder Preference Tests show that I'm cut out to be a psychiatrist, a stockbroker, or a real-estate tycoon."

"Three kinds of swindlers," says Rita.

"Thank you," says George. "My Minnesota Multiphasic Personality Inventory shows that I am basically well adjusted, though mildly depressive. Which is understandable because, after all I'm a cat . . ."

"And cats suffer," said Rita and I.

"So what kind of cat are you?"

"I'm of the genus *catus archetypalis*, as opposed to *catus particularis*."

"Which means you're a plain old barn cat, a Heinz 57 of a cat?"

"Perceptive," sniffed George.

Rita is looking out the window across the prairie. I guess she's getting worried about Sanderson. He should have been back by now. When I left him he was jacking up the pick-up and letting it lurch forward a foot or two every time. I figured it would take a little over an hour to get clear of the water, then another twenty minutes to change the tire, and probably another hour or so for the spark plugs to dry out enough for the truck to start.

I think Rita and Sanderson, in spite of all their bad luck, really love each other. Sanderson has never been one to think very far ahead, and he does have a problem with latching onto things that don't belong to him. When he do win money on the rodeo circuit he's inclined to spend it foolishly, and he do drink too much, too often. But he is a happy drinker, and he never treat Rita or his daughter badly. There are a lot worse guys around than Sanderson Makes-room-for-them.

"So far all I've seen you do is talk smart and eat my food," says Rita to George. "Do something that a power animal's supposed to do. Do something that will make me strong, happy, famous, rich."

"It's not that simple."

"I'm sure," says Rita, giving George the baleful eye.

"I don't suppose you'd have some kitty litter?"

"I don't suppose," says Rita.

"You'll excuse me then, while I retire to the beautiful outdoors to relieve myself."

"You're excused."

Turning to me Rita says, "What do you think, Silas? Is this a bad hangover? Is your old buddy, Etta, sitting down in the slough cackling and shaking like four hundred pounds of Jell-o?"

Staring out the window, trying to come up with some kind of answer, I notice some movement about a quarter-mile down the road.

"That must be Sanderson."

"Thank goodness," says Rita. "You know, life may be pretty bad with Sanderson, but it'd be worse without him."

We watch the figure make its way up the road to the gate and then on toward the house. As he gets closer we can see that Sanderson is soaked from head to foot, his clothing and hair covered in thick mud. Even though he's been on a forty-minute walk, he's still wet.

"Jesus, what a mess," says Rita.

"He must have had some serious trouble with the truck," I say.

"I'm glad to see you," says Rita as we meet him at the door. "If you weren't covered in so much guck, I'd give you a hug. So what happened?"

"Son of a bitch of a truck tipped on me. Fucking near killed me. About half an hour after Silas left, the jack went over sideways, the fender pinned me right under the water."

Sanderson pulls his mud-caked work-shirt out of his pants, lifts it up and shows us a big, semicircular bruise and scrape along his left side. "It wouldn't surprise me if a couple of ribs was broken." He holds his left hand to the sore spot.

"Take your clothes off here on the doorstep," says Rita. "Take a shower and I'll see what I can do to put medicine on that scrape. Maybe I'll have to walk down to Gloria Lefthand's and phone somebody we know with a car so we can take you to the hospital in Wetaskiwin."

"Phone's cut off again, eh?"

"Day before yesterday. They got this thing about if you don't pay the bill they turn it off." Rita laughs her good-natured laugh and shrugs to show there is worse things than having your phone disconnected.

"Hey," Sanderson say, "I just want to give you a big hug and a kiss. That's all I was thinking about as I was walking all the way here."

Rita grin, and laugh happy.

"Take off that shirt, then I'll kiss you."

Sanderson Makes-room-for-them is just about to unbutton his shirt when George the Cat amble around the corner of the house.

"What are you doing here?" George says to Sanderson.

Sanderson doesn't appear to hear or see George.

"You ain't gonna believe this, Sanderson, but that scruffy excuse for a cat is supposed to be my power animal."

"What cat?" says Sanderson, staring right at George.

George stiffens his back, his ratty hair doing its best to stand on end. His rat-chewed ears stand straight out from his head. George hisses and screeches like he just found three strange cats in his own private dumpster.

"What are you guys talkin' about?" says Sanderson.

Before we can do anything, George coils and springs, landing with his back feet on Sanderson's chest, a paw hooked on each ear, his burr-infested belly blocking off Sanderson's face.

It is now Sanderson's turn to scream.

He turn and run a few steps down the path, swatting at George every step.

"What the fuck is he doing?" yells Rita. "Do something, Silas."

Sanderson is running toward the road, wildly, like a person on fire. He is screeching, cursing, swatting, but George is now fastened on the back of Sanderson's neck.

"I'll shoot the son of a bitch," yells Rita.

She pushes me out of the way and runs into the house. She comes back in about thirty seconds with a single-shot .22 rifle and a handful of cartridges which spill as she tries to stuff them in the front pocket of her jeans.

Sanderson is all the way to the gate and on his way down the road, running full out, still yelling and swatting.

Rita aims.

"Better not," I say. "Unless you got the eye of an eagle. What do you suppose got into George?"

"He must of mistook Sanderson for somebody else."

"Could it have been Sanderson he was waiting for?"

"Not likely. He's just a goddamned barn cat."

"Should we go after them?"

"When Sanderson gets to where the ditches are full of water he can leap in, that will get rid of the cat. Cats hate water."

Rita lays the gun on the top step. "I better find me the mercurochrome bottle. Sanderson is gonna look like he been picking blackberries from the inside of the briarpatch out."

Rita ain't much of a walker. We make our way slowly down the gravel road toward where Sanderson left his truck. It took me forty minutes to walk to the house, but it take us a lot longer going back, as Rita like to stop and rest and have one of my cigarettes every little while.

Finally we come over a little rise, where we can see Sanderson's truck in the deep ditch, but there is also an RCMP car there with its blue and red lights whirling, and what looks like an ambulance is just pulling away in the direction of Highway 2 and Wetaskiwin.

Though we try to hurry, it is most of a mile to the truck. When we get there we find my friend Constable Greer sitting in his RCMP cruiser, writing notes on a clipboard. Constable Greer is gentle and friendly as an old dog, which he kind of resembles, and he knows that rules is meant to be expanded, and most of the time broken.

"Rita," Constable Greer says when he sees us, "Sanderson is okay. He got his ribs banged up pretty badly, and he needs X-rays to be sure there's no internal damage."

"We know," says Rita, which draws a quizzical look from Constable Greer, who chooses to ignore it and go on with his explanation.

"Sanderson was trying to jack the truck into shallower water when the jack tipped and pinned him down. He said he figured himself for a goner. But some stranger came walking by and pulled his head above water. Sanderson says it was a big man with red hair and green eyes, called himself George. He says George wasn't strong enough to move the truck, but eventually he shifted Sanderson enough that he could get a grip on the bumper and keep his own head above water.

"Then, as near as we can figure, this George walked over to the highway and flagged down a car, told them about the accident and to call us and an ambulance as soon as they could."

Rita and I just stare at each other.

"Did you and Sanderson have a big fight or something?" Constable Greer ask Rita.

"No," says Rita.

"Sanderson's face was cut and scratched, like he'd been wrestling in a bag full of bobcats. A real mess. But he couldn't remember how it happened to him. I guess he was in shock," says Constable Greer. "I was holding him above the water while the ambulance people were getting the truck off him, and he said he had the strangest dream while he thought he was dying.

"He said he dreamed he got free from the truck and walked all the way up to your place, because he wanted to give you one last kiss before he died. But he said just as he was reaching for you, Rita, he felt like he walked into a buzz saw, and next thing he knew this fellow George was holding his head above water, and pushing at the truck with his legs.

Constable Greer eventually gave us a ride to Wetaskiwin Hospital.

"That is the weirdest story I ever heard," says Rita, as soon as we're out of the car.

"Do you think it could have really happened?" I say. "Do you think that wasn't really Sanderson came to your place, but his spirit? And George the Cat had to drive him back to the scene of the wreck in order to save his life?"

"I don't want to think about it," says Rita.

"You should," says a voice from the marigold bed.

George the Cat appears, tail straight up in greeting, looking like he just crawled out of a wet, muddy ditch.

"You really are my power animal?"

"Never underestimate your run-of-the-mill barn cat."

"Thank you," says Rita. She reach down and pet George's head.

"Just doing my job. To add to my other excellent qualities, I'm also modest."

"I see that. What can I do for you? Do you need a home? I'll buy cat food. I'll take you to the vet for a complete overhaul. You can sleep on the sofa. I won't bitch about cat hair."

"A can of salmon would be nice. Red salmon. Then I'll be on my way."

"That's all?"

"Well, if you ever need me, I'll be around. Just think hard on me. And a little fresh meat just outside the back door wouldn't be a bad incentive."

Rita feels in the pockets of her jeans.

"All I got is twenty cents and some cartridges."

"Don't look at me," I say. "I been broke for longer than I can remember."

"Not to worry," says George the Cat. "After all, I'm a cat . . ."

". . . and cats suffer," we all three say.

Conflicting Statements

Based loosely on a Japanese folktale

"What we have here, Silas, are conflicting statements," Constable Greer say to me, shuffle a bunch of white paper covered in black typewriting. Some of the sheets been stapled together at the corners. There look to be five or six sets, some only two sheets, some more.

I stopped by the RCMP office 'cause Constable Greer always gives free coffee, and because for an RCMP he is a nice man. Because he is nice, he's made it almost to retirement age without ever being promoted. His hair is gray, his shoulders a bit stooped, and he have sad pouches under his eyes like an old dog.

The conflicting statements that he have on his desk have to do with what everyone thinks was a murder here on the reserve a couple of weeks ago. Ain't nobody been arrested for it yet, and there is as many rumors going around as dandelions growing on hillsides.

"You know, Silas, I don't believe for a minute that you came by just because you like to drink this swill we call coffee," Constable

Greer say. "In fact, I'd bet," and he sort of smile at me over top of his blue-rimmed glasses, "that a bunch of your friends suggested you stop in to see what you could find out about 'The Matter of Charles Alphonse White Pheasant.' Might be that the old medicine woman insisted that you come and see me?"

"You could be right," I say. "This coffee ain't very good. I've tasted moonshine don't burn as much on its way down."

"And the old woman?"

"Mad Etta? She's out front, sitting on her tree-trunk chair in the back of Louis Coyote's pick-up truck. But really, we was just driving by when I remembered I'd like some coffee." I smile at him when I say that.

"Well, Silas," say Constable Greer, stare around to make sure we is alone, though it is obvious the RCMP office is empty at this time of night. "I can't see that it would do any harm for you to read the statements we have on file. Might even do some good if you and Etta were to quiet some of the speculation going on. This is a strange case, but the rumors I've been hearing are twice as strange as the facts."

"Ain't that always the way," I say as he hand the papers across the desk to me. The office smell of paper and floor wax, burned coffee and something sweet, maybe that liquid soap they have in the washrooms.

"If one of my young colleagues should come in, you hand it all back real quick, start drinking your coffee, and tell me about the next book you're going to write."

The first page is headed: "Statement of Fulton Firstrider." Fulton Firstrider is a cousin of my friends Rufus and Eathen. He is about eighteen, and don't go to school, work, or do much of nothing.

I was the one who found the body.

It was Tuesday morning and I woke up about six o'clock and decided to go berrying before the sun got too hot. Yeah, if you say it was August tenth, it was August tenth. I know it was Tuesday because I watched "Cagney and Lacey" on the TV the night before.

I got me a galvanized pail, put on my straw hat and headed for the blueberry muskeg. It's about two miles straight west of where I live. Of course that's the Hobbema Reserve, where do you think? One of my little brothers woke up and tagged along, even though I told him it would be too hot for him out there.

There was heavy dew on the grass and our cuffs and shoes was soaked by the time we got to the blueberry swamp. At the front edge of the muskeg, just to the right of the best berrying spot, there is a small grove of white birch trees. Maybe it was because there was a no-good smell in the air, maybe because there was a two-gallon Gainers lard pail on its side at the edge of the blueberry patch, but I decided to walk into that grove. I told my kid brother to watch my pail and pushed through the willows and into the little clearing.

That's where I found the body.

No, there was no weapon. No gun.

I recognize the guy laying there as Charlie White Pheasant. He's married to Leona Carbine, who's a cousin of mine. He might be my cousin too, everybody around here is somebody's cousin.

Charlie was laying on his side and it easy to see he been shot through the chest. His shirt was soaked with blood, dried. Didn't look as if he was still bleeding, though him and the grass around him was wet with dew. His mouth was hanging open, his lips pulled back from his teeth. His lips had dried blood on them, his teeth looked dry, and there was big green flies crawling on his mouth.

No. I didn't touch him at all. I was scared. I just stood and stared for a few seconds, then I heard my kid brother pushing his way through the willows. I didn't want him to see the body, so I ran to meet him and led him back to the berry patch.

"I want you to run back to town," I told him. "Go to where the phone is at Hobbema General Store. If Ben Stonebreaker ain't opened up yet, pound on the back door until you wake him. Tell him to call the RCMP. When they come, you lead them out here." He took off.

Yes, the grass in the clearing was bent and flattened, asters and tiger lilies was broke down. Looked to me like there might have been a good fight.

Right beside the body I seen a leather thong, a long thin one, the kind loggers use to lace their boots.

I suppose there might have been two, but I only seen one. Only other thing I seen was a bright red button in the grass, look like it come off my cousin Leona's red western shirt.

How do I know that? Cause I'd seen Leona walking around the last couple of days in a red shirt with red buttons.

The next statement was from Flora Snakeskin, who is about fifteen, live in a shack between Hobbema town and the blueberry muskeg.

> I seen them about noon the day before. That's right, Monday the ninth. I seen Charlie and Leona heading off to go berrying. No, I didn't talk to them. They were carrying a bucket, that's how I know.
>
> Clothes? She had on a silk western shirt, bright red, with a white fringe on the shoulders and across the back. I wish I had an old man who'd buy me a shirt like that. Leona was lucky to have a good husband.
>
> Charlie? He wore a creamy-colored shirt, short-sleeved, I think. They were both wearing jeans.
>
> A gun? Well, sure, Charlie always carried a gun, a sawed-off .22. He had it stuck in his belt. He shot crows and magpies for bounty and squirrels for food.
>
> Hey, if people didn't do nothin' illegal, you guys would be out of a job, right?
>
> Nah, Leona didn't do any shooting. At least I never seen her. But Charlie could pick a sparrow off a willow tree from clear across a slough.

Constable Chrétien's report was headed: "Statement of Constable Luc Pierre Chrétien."

> On the afternoon of Wednesday the eleventh, I brought the suspect, Edward Raymond Wolffinder, in for questioning. He is known as "Big Eddie" Wolffinder, first of all because he is big. I would esti-

mate six-foot-two and 220 pounds. He also has a young brother, age perhaps six, who is known as "Little Eddie," and a cousin called "Black Eddie" Wolffinder.

Big Eddie had only recently returned to the reserve after serving a term in Fort Saskatchewan jail. He accosted a young couple parked in an isolated spot on the reserve. He pulled the man from the car and assaulted him, then reportedly sexually assaulted the woman. At trial there was some question as to how much co-operation he received from the woman — she was an ex-girlfriend of his — so he was acquitted of the sexual assault charge and convicted of assault causing bodily harm.

Edward Raymond Wolffinder is known to law-enforcement personnel as a dangerous and volatile person.

That afternoon I found him drinking in the Alice Hotel beer parlor in Wetaskiwin, and asked him to accompany me to the RCMP headquarters to answer some questions. He was quite co-operative, even boastful, and gave a statement of his own free will. He freely admitted being in the company of Charles and Leona White Pheasant on the day in question.

Our foremost concern was to discover the where-abouts of Leona White Pheasant. At that time she had been missing for over forty-eight hours. By questioning Mr. Wolffinder, we hoped to establish if Mrs. White Pheasant was still alive or, if not, the location of her body.

He did not have a gun in his possession, though he carried a hunting knife in a sheath on his belt.

Statement of Nellie Carbine, taken Wednesday, August eleventh.

Yes, Leona White Pheasant is my daughter. Last time I seen her was three or four days ago. She's eighteen and been married to Charlie for about a year. He's five years older than her, but a nice guy. He's never raised up his hand to her that I know of, though it wouldn't surprise me if she give him cause sometimes. I was glad when they decided to get married, Leona been a big worry to me.

Well, Leona's young and pretty and, even if she is my daughter, a silly girl. She been awfully wild all her teens. If you ask me, she was real lucky not to have two or three babies by now. Charlie's a good guy, kind of serious, not very handsome. He had to take Leona on the rodeo circuit with him 'cause he couldn't trust her to behave herself at home on her own. I was sorry about Leona being like that.

I'm real sorry something happened to Charlie. I hate to think I might lose them both. I hope you catch whoever done it.

Statement of Big Eddie Wolffinder.

I killed Charlie, sort of, but not Leona. I don't know what's become of her. Honest. Hell, if I'd wasted them both I'd tell you. What have I got to lose?

I'd been staying with my cousin, Ignace Cardinal. I'd just got up, must have been about noon, and was gonna walk down to Hobbema Pool Hall and hang out until evening, when I met Charlie and Leona on the trail. They were off to go berrying. Leona hit me up for a cigarette and we got to talking and laughing. Pretty soon I was walking with them toward the berry patch. I'd seen Leona around a couple of times and kind of had my eye on her. I also knew she was trouble. She's one of those women who know how to be sexy, she could let a guy know with just one glance that she was available.

She was wearing a western shirt, silky-smooth, unbuttoned until almost all her tits showed. She not wearing a thing under that shirt. Her jeans are tight and sexy and there's a rip in one knee. Charlie wasn't very friendly, but I never let that bother me before. I knew after we all been together about two minutes that I was gonna have that sexy girl that day.

I'm a guy who always takes what he wants. I knew all I had to do was wait until some time when Charlie was away or when Leona was in town alone, but I had to have her right then.

When we got to the berry patch this grove of birch trees just past a willow-stand give me an idea.

"Hey, Charlie," I said. "Yesterday I left a bottle of moonshine stashed out under one of them birches. Let's go have ourselves a drink."

He looked like he didn't trust me, but finally he said okay. Guess he was glad to get me away from Leona. I think we both been making it pretty clear we was hot for each other.

"You start picking berries," I said to Leona, "and

when we get back we gonna check your mouth make sure it ain't blue, make sure you're picking more than you're eating." I winked at her, and she lick her lips and smile sexy.

Charlie walk ahead of me, push through the willows to the clearing. Soon as we got there, I reached around and grabbed the gun out of his belt. He was scared.

"I ain't gonna hurt you," I said. Couldn't find a thing, so I made him sit down while I unlaced one of my boots, then I tied his hands with the long leather lace. I made him put his legs one on each side of a birch sapling, and I used the second lace to tie his ankles so's he couldn't go no place.

Then I called out to Leona, "Come here! Have a shot of moonshine with us." I held the gun on Charlie to let him know I'd shoot him if he warned her. I dunno if I would of or not. Probably. I wanted her awful bad.

What she saw as she came into the clearing was Charlie tied up on the far side and me grinning at her and holding the gun. It was a dirty thing to do to both of them, but I wanted to show off. I wanted him to see how hot she was for me. I wanted her so hot for me she'd do it right in front of her husband.

I sure was surprised at what happened next.

"You son of a bitch," she said, and mean as you please kicked me in the shin. She had on pointed cowboy boots, the kind they make for women. It hurt like hell.

Here, let me show you the bruise. Look at that, still all swelled up. Looks like when we used to get drunk and have shin-kicking contests when I worked winters in the lumber camp.

I tossed the gun out of everybody's reach and grabbed onto Leona. The button holding her tits in popped off her shirt, almost hit me in the eye. I forced her down on the grass. She was fighting like a bitch, had to sit on her to pull her boots and jeans off. She was scratching at me like a bobcat. We did it then.

Yes, intercourse. What the hell you think, played checkers? I'm a good man, let me tell you. After a while she forgot she was mad at me. She moaned and cried and dug her nails into my back. She was enjoying herself.

When I was finished with her, I just figured I'd keep the gun and head on my way. I'd take my chances they wouldn't call in the Horsemen.

But while we was pulling on our clothes, she whisper to me, "What am I gonna do? He'll never live with me again. You shamed us both, you bastard. Why couldn't you wait?"

I didn't say anything.

"Fight him!" she hissed. "If he wins he'll take me back. If you win I'll be your old lady." She sure did look beautiful, tucking her red shirt in her jeans, her hair all wild and smeared across her face.

I know it's hard to understand but I believed what she said. And I wanted her more than I ever wanted anything. I'd have killed as many people as I had to to make that girl mine.

I walked across the clearing, untied Charlie's feet,

put the lace in my pocket. As I undid his hands, I said, "We'll fight. Whoever gets the gun uses it." He nodded. When I finished untying his hands I let the bootlace fall to the ground because he butted me in the belly and knocked the wind out of me. He kicked me in the face as I went down.

He sprang right over me and got to the gun. He could have shot me in the body, but he wanted to shoot me in the head, so he came in close. I hooked my right foot behind him and pulled him down, grabbing his arm as I did. We wrestled all across the clearing. I tell you, I'm a hell of a fistfighter but I never fought anybody as tough. I gradually bent his arm back until the gun was pointing at him. Then I gave his arm a real sharp pull and the gun shot him in the chest.

He slumped to the ground. There was blood in the corner of his mouth, and his breath come short and noisy like a dying animal. The gun fall out of his hand and lay on the ground. Then he gasped and his eyes rolled back in his head.

I turned toward Leona, but she was gone. I rushed to the berry patch, but she wasn't there either. I stood and listened but I couldn't hear a sound. I don't have any idea what became of her. I didn't kill her. I'd never kill her.

The next statement was on a different colored sheet of paper and was taken at RCMP Headquarters in a town called Rimbey, maybe forty miles west of Hobbema. An RCMP Constable Doerksen found Leona White Pheasant wandering, incoherent and suffering from exposure, not far from Rimbey, on the morning of Thursday, August 12, three days after she was last seen at Hobbema.

The first two pages of her statement don't tell anything that I ain't heard already, but the rest was new.

When Eddie was through with me and while we were both pulling on our clothes, I tried not to look at my husband, all tied up there and having to see what was happening to me. I sure hoped Eddie wasn't going to kill us now that he'd got what he wanted. But he hardly looked at either of us, just buckled up his belt and walked off toward the berry patch, never once looking back.

I stumbled over to Charlie, and, oh, the look on his face was something terrible to see. That look scared me half to death, told me he blamed me, wanted to kill me.

"It wasn't my fault," I whispered. He never spoke one word. His eyes were just dead full of hate for me.

I went over and picked up Charlie's gun from where Eddie had tossed it. I cocked it and put it up against my head, right in front of my ear.

"I'll kill myself if you tell me to," I said. "Just say it."

Charlie stared at me for quite a few seconds. Then he said, in a dull voice that didn't even sound like him, "Kill me first." I could tell that he meant it. There was so much pain in his eyes.

"I'll join you, I promise," I said.

I put the gun barrel against the center of his chest,

and, looking away, I pulled the trigger. He slumped over on his side. His breath made kind of a gargling sound in his throat.

A .22 holds only one bullet. I looked in all Charlie's pockets, he always carried bullets, but I couldn't find any. Maybe he forgot to bring some, maybe Eddie made him hand them over, I don't know.

I was screaming, I was so angry. I threw the gun on the ground. Then I saw that Charlie was still tied up. I couldn't leave him like that. I untied his hands and feet.

I guess I went crazy then. I wanted to kill myself, I'd promised Charlie. I was going to run until I dropped. Then I came to a creek. I tried to drown myself, but the water wasn't deep enough. I hit myself on the head with a rock. You can see the bruises, and there's a cut in my hair there. But I didn't die. I hoped maybe a bear would find me, but even that didn't happen. I was out for a couple of nights before this trapper found me and took me to the RCMP.

I don't know what's going to happen to me. I killed my husband, and I promised to follow.

What we know now was that, even though he looked like a corpse when Fulton Firstrider found him, Charlie White Pheasant wasn't dead. Constable Bobowski of the RCMP answered the call. It was her who felt Charlie's neck for a pulse, and when she found one radioed for an ambulance: the ambulance guys had to carry him on a stretcher for almost half a mile, 'cause that's as close as any trail come to the blueberry muskeg.

Charlie didn't regain consciousness until Thursday morning, about the time that trapper was finding Leona forty or fifty miles away. He was only awake for twenty minutes. Constable Greer recorded his statement at the Wetaskiwin Hospital. Charlie died that afternoon, without ever knowing what had become of Leona.

Again, the first few pages of Charlie's statement said the same things I already heard, but then he add some surprising stuff.

When he grabbed my gun I figured he was going to kill me. But instead he tied me up and called for Leona to come into the clearing.

Then he raped Leona. He went on with her for a long time. I couldn't make myself look but from the noises they made I think Leona got to liking it. I mean she's young and wild, and once she forgot that he started out by forcing her . . .

When they were finished and putting on their clothes, he was talking away to her just like they were old friends. Even though I couldn't hear all that was said, I know I heard Leona laugh once, and that broke my heart open. I always been mad-jealous of her, but I loved her more than anything. I'd have always stuck by her. But I guess she didn't care.

Big Eddie was saying, "Now that you been with a real man, you won't ever be satisfied with nobody but me."

I could have been yelling all along, but I got my pride. Everything was my fault anyway, for letting Big Eddie trick me. I only said one thing. "Don't believe him!" That was all.

Then I heard Leona's answer, and my heart really broke open in my chest.

"Yeah," she said, and paused that way she has, and I knew she was giving him a sexy smile. "I think I might like being your old lady."

Just as her and Eddie was ready to leave, her hanging onto his hand like it was them that was married, she stopped dead still and glanced across at me, really looked at me for the first time since all this happened.

"Kill him!" she said to Big Eddie. "I don't want him telling around what I done, giving me a bad name. Shoot him!" And she yelled that three or four times, hanging like a spoiled kid on Eddie's arm, begging him to kill me.

I felt so empty. I wouldn't put up a fight. If Eddie wanted to kill me, okay.

Eddie stared at her, and he stared at me, and all of a sudden he slapped her hard, once on the forehead, once on the side of the head. She went down, rolled over, and sat up, stunned and crying, there was blood on her forehead.

"What do you want me to do with her?" Eddie asked me. "Just say the word." And stared down at her with a mean face.

"Leave her for me," I said.

When she heard that Leona sprang up and staggered through the willows toward the muskeg.

Soon as she was gone, Eddie walked over to me, his shoulders kind of slumped. He took his knife out of its sheath and cut the bootlace on my wrists. While I untied my feet he turned and walked slowly away.

When I was sure he was gone I picked up my gun, put the barrel against my chest and shot myself. A long time later, when everything was dark, I hear someone come back. I opened my eyes but it was still dark, like I was blindfolded. But I could feel someone pry my fingers off the gun.

"This is all?" I say to Constable Greer. "I mean who done what to who? Ain't you cops supposed to figure out the answer?"

"Sometimes there aren't any answers," says Constable Greer.

Dream Catcher

Delores won't talk about it with me, or my friend Frank Fencepost, or even Joseph, our brother who's retarded. "Developmentally delayed" they call Joseph now, like he's a bus that's not on schedule.

Delores won't talk to us because we're male. She's talked some to Ma, but not a lot. And when she wake up every night at two or three in the morning, crying and screaming, she don't let no one but Ma hold her.

What happened to Delores wasn't as bad as it could of been, but Bedelia Coyote, who works down at the Rape Crisis Center in Wetaskiwin, say it how bad Delores feels that is the important thing. And Delores feel really bad.

She was attacked right here on the reserve, not two hundred yards from home. She'd been down at Blue Quills Hall rehearsing with Molly Thunder's dance troupe, the Duck Lake Massacre. Delores, when she perform, is all decked out in blue and red feathers and beaded buckskins. She use finger cymbals, clatter and stomp around the stage like a prairie chicken strut.

Delores was wearing jeans and a New Kids on the Block T-shirt; she carried her costume in a plastic Safeway grocery bag. She was heading up the hill from Blue Quills Hall toward home at about ten o'clock of a September Saturday night.

The guy who attacked her was somebody Delores knowed all her life, Ovide Lafrenierre, who live with his grandmother, Bertha Crossbow, in a purple-and-white Indian Affairs cabin just down the road from our place.

Ovide is about eighteen, but none of us know him very well. Dropped out of school when he was fourteen, been watching TV or playing video games from the Wetaskiwin library ever since.

He is a polite-looking boy with neat water-combed hair and hunched-up shoulders, a slight build, and brown eyes that look off over your shoulder if you talk to him. He usually wear a black corduroy jacket, black jeans, a black T-shirt, and he don't have any friends that I know of.

What Delores told Ma was that while she was walking home, she heard footsteps on the trail behind her. She figured it was me or Frank or some other neighbor. She didn't pay much attention, even when the footsteps got real close. Then somebody throw an arm around her neck, drag her down the hill into the tall grass and bullrushes of the slough, which in September is so dry the grass is crackly-brown, bullrushes ripe and soft as a horse's nose.

Delores say the person don't speak at all, but she recognize the feel of the black jacket because it is the only one like it on the reserve, plus Ovide Lafrenierre always got the warm odor of cinnamon gum about him. The moon so bright it almost like daylight, so she can tell it is Ovide soon as he turn her around and start pulling at her clothes. Delores may be only twelve but she is a lot stronger than she look. She been dancing since she was a little girl and the muscles of her legs is birch-hard. She also took karate lessons for a while and one time let go a spin kick that accidentally hit Frank in his private parts.

Frank had been teasing Delores and had hidden some of the beer bottles she collect from alongside the highway, which is why Delores is known as the Bottle Queen. All Delores intend to do was kick the cigarette out of Frank's hand, but Frank move right into the kick, squeal like a pig just had its throat cut, double up on the floor, and groan. Frank claim the world going to be deprived of any more little Fenceposts, say that he gonna have Delores charged with libel and slander, which are words he read in one of my book contracts, assault causing bodily harm, and illegal possession of lethal feet.

As Ovide Lafrenierre split her T-shirt all the way down the front, Delores kick him on the right kneecap and scream, "No! No!" loud as she can, just like she been taught at a class Bedelia Coyote and Constable B.B. Bobowski of the RCMP held in the school basement one winter.

In the clear fall air her voice carry all the way to Blue Quills Hall, and a few people there start up the hill toward her scream. Her kick to the knee knock Ovide down, but he pull Delores with him. She make her right hand stiff and poke Ovide three times in the neck, make him let out a howl, break free, and go limping off up the hill.

I been known to make a lot of fun of the RCMP, but they handle everything about Delores' case quick and efficient. Me and Ma and Delores ride in Constable Greer's patrol car all the way to Wetaskiwin, where he phone to get Constable Bobowski down to

RCMP headquarters. It being a Saturday night, she was in a frilly dress with a white shawl over her shoulders. I hardly recognize her without her RCMP hat, with her blonde hair hanging loose over her shoulders.

Constable Bobowski take Delores into her office and keep her there for over an hour. She come out a couple of times, whisper to Constable Greer. Constable Greer strap on his gun, which usually live like a weasel in the bottom drawer of his desk, say he driving back to the reserve to arrest the perpetrator.

"As long as he get Ovide Lafrenierre, I don't care who else he arrest," Ma say to me in Cree.

When Constable Greer bring him in, at four in the morning, Ovide don't look very dangerous, just a skinny, sleepy-eyed little wimp with a bad knee. He can't raise no bail so have to stay in jail for the three months until his trial.

When Delores get called to testify, they clear the courtroom even of me and Ma.

At home that night, Delores tell as much as she can remember. She say both the lawyers were nice to her. The prosecutor lawyer was a pale young fellow look like he should still be in high school. Ovide's lawyer, a good-looking Indian guy, come all the way from Calgary.

That defence lawyer ask if she knew Ovide before, and if they ever talked or visited, and if he ever tried to do anything to her before. Then he ask if Delores ever played with Ovide, and Delores say that a few times when she was younger Ovide been outside playing with her and her friends, and that they all kick a soccer ball around, and that they might have played tag or kick-the-can.

"Did you ever wrestle with Ovide Lafrenierre?" the lawyer ask.

"Well, sort of," Delores tell him. "One time Ovide chased us little kids around, pretending he was a bear and was going to eat us up."

"And did he wrestle you to the ground?"

"Yes."

"And was it all in fun? Or were you afraid of him?"

"It was all in fun."

"At that time did Ovide Lafrenierre hurt you in any way?"

"No."

"Isn't it possible that when on the night in question Ovide Lafrenierre put his arm around you and tried to wrestle you down, he was just continuing the game?"

"I don't think so," Delores answer.

"But you're not sure?"

"It was different."

"How?"

"It wasn't the same."

"Can you tell me how it was different?"

"He was going to hurt me."

"Did he say he was going to hurt you?"

"No."

Delores say the lawyer keep asking those same questions, in different words, for a long, long time.

That defence lawyer call up as a witness Ben Stonebreaker who run the general store on the reserve.

"How many packages of cinnamon gum do you sell in a week?" he ask Ben.

"Thirty or forty," Ben answer.

Then he call a person from the company that make the jacket Ovide was wearing.

"How many of these jackets did your company manufacture?"

The fellow look at a computer page he got in his hand.

"Three thousand."

"And during what period of time were they shipped to retail stores?"

The fellow explain they started to manufacture them three years before, ship the last of them six months ago.

"How many were shipped to stores in Alberta?"

The man consult his computer page. "One thousand, nine hundred, approximately."

"No further questions," say the lawyer.

Ovide's grandmother, Bertha Crossbow, need a Cree-speaking translator because she is an old-fashioned Indian lady, wear a long, dark skirt and matching babushka, and never spoke a word of English in her life. I guess, like most older Indian people, she figure any white-man oath don't mean a thing, so she only say things that be good for Ovide's side.

Mrs. Crossbow say Ovide been a good boy all his life, never in no trouble and so shy he don't want to leave home, even though he was one time offered a job as a clerk in a video store in Wetaskiwin.

Then she swear that Ovide was home with her the night he attacked Delores. She say she sat in the kitchen all night listen to the singing sounds of Ovide's video games, and that Ovide never left the house even for one minute.

"There ain't enough evidence to convict," the judge say.

Ovide is free to go home.

We decide to make a social call on Ovide Lafrenierre.

"We ain't gonna do him no physical harm," say Frank, after his girl Connie Bigcharles say she's afraid we gonna get ourselves in trouble. "Guy like Ovide ain't as valuable as roadkill."

Out of the darkness at the back of her cabin, Etta sit high up on her tree-trunk chair, sip from a bottle of Lethbridge Pale Ale. The light from the coal-oil lamp glint off the rim of the bottle, amber as a cat's eye.

"There are other ways of dealing with him," Etta say.

Delores was waking up only once a night instead of two or three times, but Ovide was back living right near us, and Delores say she don't want to go out of the house at all. Ma has to walk her to school and back. And instead of bouncing into the cabin all pink-faced from the cold weather, Delores stay in her room, don't even have friends over to play.

One day after Frank fire up his Poulan chainsaw he take a few whacks at a spruce stump behind his cabin. Then he take a few more, and before long that stump look like a face, and before long it isn't just any face, but Chief Tom Crow-eye, complete with the sullen smirk we all love to hate.

Frank could probably make some money from his talent. Some guys carve out animal shapes from big chunks of tree trunk at flea markets and the opening of auto dealerships. Trouble is, what Frank carve best is little men with penises big as their bodies. Self-portraits, Frank call them. Frank been chased off from a craft fair or two because his art embarrass the old white ladies who come to buy Depression glass or velvet pillows with the face of Jesus or Elvis in sequins.

About eight o'clock one night a dozen or so of us, including

Bedelia Coyote, gather in front of Old Lady Crossbow's cabin. Frank fire up the chainsaw which belch out blue smoke and make the air stink of oil and gas.

Eventually, she peek out a window then come to the door.

"Send Ovide out," we say.

"What you gonna do to him?"

We feel a little sorry for the old lady. One of her daughters gone off to the city, had Ovide, then died of drinking Lysol or huffing WD-40. The welfare brought Ovide to Mrs. Crossbow when he was about four, said he been abused something awful. Old Lady Crossbow didn't have to take him, but she did. Ain't her fault he grown up to be a pervert.

"We want him to watch a demonstration," says Bedelia. "We won't hurt him. But if he don't come out we'll come in and get him."

Mrs. Crossbow go away for a long time. If there was a back door Ovide would have been long gone, but there ain't. So after a long while she bring Ovide to the door, though he stand behind her and look as if he wish he was far away.

"You don't need to be scared of us *tonight*," Bedelia say.

Frank step forward, the belching chainsaw in one hand, a crooked piece of tamarack, with a foot and a leg from the knee down carved out in the other.

"Just in case you ever get the urge to attack another girl the way you did Delores Ermineskin," Frank say, "here's what gonna happen. We'll come round for a visit in the middle of the night, truss you up like a bundle of oats, and whittle little pieces off you like this."

Frank hold up the tamarack leg, touch the blade to the foot part, and the little toe go spinning down onto the ground.

One by one, Frank amputate the toes.

"When the toes are all gone we take off pieces of your foot about an inch at a time. When we get up to your knee, we start on the other leg."

Even though he ain't bleeding, Ovide Lafrenierre get paler by the minute.

"We'll take our time. Etta be there to stop the bleeding, make sure you stay awake to enjoy the show. We wouldn't want you to get off easy and die."

Etta wave a big hand at Ovide, let him know Frank ain't just making things up.

"You getting the picture?" Bedelia ask Ovide.

He nod.

"I seen healthier looking dead people," says Bedelia, as we walk away.

It is Etta who bring the dream catcher to our cabin.

"I got something for Delores," she say to me when I stop by her place on my way home from the Tech School. She suggest I drive her over to our place. When Etta suggest something it is good as law.

A dream catcher been hanging on the curtain of Etta's cabin for years and years but I figure it is mostly superstition.

The dream catcher Etta bring for Delores is fresh made from a red willow sapling, bent into a circle about four inches across. The ends are sewed together and heavy thread criss-cross the circle make a web kind of like a volleyball net. They says if you hang a dream catcher by your bedroom window it will catch the bad dreams and the good dreams will slip through the holes.

Almost ever since she was attacked, Delores go to see a

counselor in Wetaskiwin once a week, talk with this lady about how she feel, but those sessions don't seem to be doing much good. Delores is still depressed, frightened, wake every night crying, and don't leave our cabin unless she forced to.

"I figure we've given all this talk stuff enough of a chance," says Etta. She go into Delores' bedroom, stay a long time, talking softly to Delores.

It been two weeks now since Etta fastened the dream catcher on the curtain by Delores' bed. The first night I got up and checked on her a couple of times, the way I been doing every night. She was tossing and turning a lot, had the sheet all wound around two or three times, whimpered some, but she didn't once wake up crying and frightened the way she usually do.

By the end of a week I don't have to check on her no more. She sleeps calm on her back with her head on the pillow, the covers hardly disturbed at all, a little bump about halfway down the bed where her feet stick up.

During the daytime Delores is happier, too. She invite Tanya Little Circle over to play Barbie dolls, and she laugh and shriek with her friend the way she used to. She even getting to like me and Joseph again. The other morning she give me a hug around the neck like she always did, and I seen her cuddled up in Joseph's lap.

"It worked," I tell Etta.

Etta just stare at me, raise one of her old, gray eyebrows maybe half an inch, let me know there was never a doubt, and that she is a little annoyed I feel I have to report back to her.

What Etta do admit to me later on, while she boil us up some cocoa on her big cookstove, is that there is also a dream catcher can hold on to the good dreams only, let the bad ones slip through.

"Did you?" I ask.

Etta let me know by her expression this don't deserve an answer either.

I notice then, that even in the dull light of Etta's coal-oil lamp, with a wick that always burn crooked at one corner, there are scratches across Etta's cheeks and forehead, look like she been in a bag with a bobcat. And the backs of her hands are in even worse shape.

"There is a real nasty bank of blackberry vines behind Old Lady Crossbow's cabin," I say. "Grow right up to that skunk's bedroom window."

Etta look at me like she just push aside a rock and there I am.

Walking home, the moon is bright as a penny in a high, clear sky. Everything is night-silent except for the occasional yelp of a lonely dog and the crackle of the Northern Lights.

At Old Lady Crossbow's house, I step stealthily across her front yard, and down the side of the cabin to the bank of blackberry vines, take a scratch on the cheek staring along the back of the house toward Ovide's bedroom.

From the window come a wild eerie sound, a nightmare clawing its way out of a throat, the cry of an animal been hurt sudden and bad. I hear the flap of an owl taking off from one of the tamarack trees behind the cabin. It look to me like the dream catcher that hang from the corner of the sash is wiggling in the moonlight though there ain't even a hint of a breeze.

Brother Frank's Gospel Hour

One of the weird things the government does for us Indians, not that everything the government does for us ain't weird in some way, is they provide money for us to have our own Indian radio station. The station is KUGH, known as K-UGH. The call letters were chosen a long time ago by Indians with a sense of humor. The white men are always a little embarrassed saying the name, so they call it K-U-G-H.

A year or so ago I read a letter in an Indian magazine, maybe it was the *Saskatchewan Indian*, where some woman was complaining, saying it was demeaning for it to be called K-UGH. One of the problems of Indians getting more involved in the everyday world is that they lose their sense of humor.

To tell the truth no one I know on the reserve pay much attention to the radio station. It originate in someplace like Yellowknife, which is about a million miles north of us, and instead of playing good solid country and loud rock 'n' roll, it is mainly talk, in a lot of dialects. It is a place for people to complain, which is the national pastime in Canada, the one thing whites and Indians, French and English, and everybody else got in common. And it seem like the smaller the minority the louder they whine.

It does have a news program called the "Moccasin Telegraph," where the title been stolen from a story I wrote quite a few years ago. People send messages to friends and relatives who are out on their traplines or who just live hundreds of miles from anywhere and they can't get to pick up their mail but once or twice a year.

"This here's to Joe and Daisy up around Mile 800. Cousin Franny's got a new baby on the eighteenth, a boy, Benjamin. Oscar wrecked his car, eh? We're doin' fine and see you in the spring. Sam and Darlene."

There would be an hour or more of messages like that run every night.

K-UGH would have gone on forever with only a few people noticing it, but somebody in the government get the idea that things got to be centralized. That way everybody get to share in the money the government waste.

First we know of it is when one morning a couple of flatdeck trucks arrive at the reserve loaded down with concrete blocks. They followed by another flatdeck with a bulldozer and three or four pick-up trucks painted dismal Ottawa government green, full of guys in hard hats who measure with tapes, look through little telescopes and tie red ribbons to willow bushes and to stakes they pound in the ground.

That first night it is like a pilgrimage from the village to the construction site, which is on the edge of a slough down near the highway. By morning almost everybody who need concrete blocks have a more than adequate supply.

People got their front porches propped up, and I bet twenty

families have concrete-block coffee tables. A couple of guys are building patios. I helped myself to a few pieces of lumber as well and my sister Delores and me made some bookshelves for the living room. Me and Delores each own about two hundred books at least, and until now they been living in boxes under our beds.

Nobody bother to tell the construction people that the place they planning to build on will disappear under about three feet of slough water when the snow melt in the spring or when we get a gully-washer of a thunderstorm, which happens about twice a week through the summer. But it is fall now and the grass is dry and crackly, and there is the smell of burning tamarack in the air, and the sun shines warm.

The construction men get awful mad about all the concrete blocks that disappear. They yell loud as school teachers, but we just stand around watching them, don't say nothing. A guy in an unscratched yellow hard hat say he going to send a truck through the village pick up every concrete block he sees.

Mad Etta, our medicine lady, stand up slowly from her tree-trunk chair, her joints cracking like kindling snapping. She waddle over to the foreman.

"You got a brand on your concrete blocks like the farmers over west of here have on their cattle?"

The foreman scratch his head. "No." And after he think a while he decide that collecting back concrete blocks ain't such a good idea. But that foreman have a long talk with someone on his cellular phone and the next load of concrete blocks have a big red R stamped on them that there is no scratching off.

"By the way," Etta say to the foreman, "what is it you're building?"

Rumors been going round that they gonna build public washrooms like they have at highway rest stops. Somebody else says the government going to build a Petro Canada service station, though the spot ain't within two miles of any kind of regular road.

"We're buildin' a twenty-by-twenty concrete-block building," says the foreman. "What they do with the building after we're finished ain't no concern of ours. Our department just build."

"I'm sure you do," says Etta, which the foreman take as positive.

The building seem too small to house anything important.

"I bet they gonna store nuclear waste, or a whole lot of these here PCBs," me and Frank say to Bedelia Coyote, knowing this will send Bedelia's blood pressure up about 100 percent. Bedelia belong to every protest group ever march with a clenched fist. She been out in British Columbia picketing the forest industry for cutting on Indian land, and down in southern Alberta trying to stop the dam on the Oldman River. Bedelia turn paranoid if you even hint somebody might be doing something not good for Indians or the environment.

"Her natural shade is green as I feel after partying all Saturday night," Frank say.

Bedelia kind of scoff but it's only a day or two until her and her friends is investigating like crazy, trying to find which government department is building the concrete-block building and for what.

"If you want something done all you got to do is delegate somebody to do it for you, even if they don't exactly understand that they been delegated," say Frank, smile his gap-toothed smile.

By the time Bedelia and her friends pin down what the building is for, a couple of flatdeck trucks is bringing in pieces of skeletal metal that eventually going to be a tall antenna with a red light on top to keep away airplanes.

"It's going to be a radio station," Bedelia shout as she crash through the door of the pool hall. "They're going to move the Indian radio station here to the reserve."

We didn't suspect it then, but those words were going to change the lives of me and my friends forever.

After the construction workers leave, a group of men in white coats arrive, unpack boxes full of electronic stuff. By peeking through the only window in the building we can see them with little soldering irons, hooking all this stuff together. There is a couple of snow-white satellite dishes set behind the building. The installers push some buttons, and the satellite dishes hum and turn, pointing their centers, which have a big stick like in the middle of a flower, at different parts of the sky.

There are boards full of flashing red, green, and blue lights that run the whole length of the building, which is divided into three cubicles, one big and two little, each one outlined by thick, clear-plastic walls.

One of Bedelia's "friends in high places," as she calls them, sends her a press release all about the Indian radio station K-UGH being moved to our reserve. It's part of a process of centralization of federal government and Department of Indian Affairs affiliates, whatever that might mean.

Painters turn up and paint the building all white on the outside (not a good sign, Bedelia says) with the call letters K-U-G-H in big green letters with red feathers, like part of a head dress, trailing off from each end.

At night we are able to receive K-UGH on our radios, but it still broadcasting from Whitehorse or Yellowknife, or one of those places with an Indian name. And it's still mainly talk and go off the air at 11:00 p.m., just when real radio listeners are waking up.

Frank, who is able to open doors by not doing much more than looking at them, let us into the radio building. Frank push every button he can reach, but nothing appear to be hooked up. We all go into the room with the microphone and Frank sit himself down in front of that microphone and pretend he is on the air.

"Good evening, all you handsome people out in radio land. This here's Frank Fencepost, a combination of whiskey, money, and great sex, all things that make people feel good, just waiting to make you happy."

"Make-up," say Frank's girl, Connie Bigcharles. "I need lots of make-up to be happy."

"A CD player," add my girl, Sadie One-wound.

"A credit card," say Rufus Firstrider.

"With no credit limit, and they never send a bill," say Rufus' big brother, Eathen Firstrider.

"And one of them Lamborzucchini cars that go about a thousand miles an hour," says Robert Coyote.

"World peace," say his sister, Bedelia.

"Boo!" we all say.

Then Frank ask the question that in just a few months will make him a little bit famous, and maybe gonna make him real famous.

"What do you need to make you happy? Tell Brother Frank, my friends. Brother Frank can make your dreams come true."

He repeat the question.

"I want you to pick up the phone, brothers and sisters. I want you to pick up a pen and write to Brother Frank in care of the station to which you are listening. I want all you wonderful people to let me know what it would take to make you happy."

"You're crazier than usual," we say to Frank.

"Thank you," says Frank. "But I think I'm on to something here. I sure wish I could figure out how to turn this equipment on. I really want to talk to people."

"Get a life," somebody says.

A few days later the radio station go on the air. One afternoon two cars pull up and park in front of the concrete-block building. A thin Indian with a braid, dressed in jeans and a denim jacket, get out of one, and a hefty Indian, look like he could be a relative of Mad Etta, get out of the other car.

"We been expecting you," Frank say, sticking out his hand to the thin Indian. "I am Fencepost, aspiring broadcast journalist. Me and my friends are at your service."

Both guys look at us real strangely. The thin one is Vince Gauthier, the announcer. The fat guy is Harvey Many Children, the engineer.

That's it. Takes just two Indians to operate K-UGH. Vince open the mail, decide which letters get read on the air. He do all the talking. Harvey make sure what Vince says gets out over the air. Other people, maybe in Edmonton or somewhere, sell advertising, fax in the commercials and the times when Vince is supposed to read them.

The station only open from 3:00 p.m. to 11:00 p.m. Monday to Friday.

"If there's a holiday, the station ain't open," Vince tell us. They can only afford two employees. When Harvey go on holidays, I have to do both jobs. You think that ain't fun . . . . When I go on holidays the station shut down for three weeks."

Vince and Harvey ain't very friendly at first, but Frank just study them and, as he says, figure their angles.

"Everybody wants something. Harvey's easy. We just bring him food. McDonald's, Kentucky Fried, chicken fried steak from Miss Goldie's Café. That will get us in the door. But Vince is the important one. I can't figure his angle yet."

It sure ruffle Frank's feathers some that I am the one Vince invite to be on the air.

"I know your name from someplace," he say to me the second day we hanging around while they is working.

"'America's Most Wanted,'" say Frank.

Vince stare Frank into the concrete floor.

"I've written a few books," I say.

"Okay, you're *that* Silas Ermineskin. How about I have you on the show tomorrow? Bring your books in and we'll talk about them. I've always meant to read one of your books, but I never got around to it."

"That's what everybody say," I tell him.

"What about talking to me?" says Frank. "I'm the one inspired Silas to write. 'Sit down at your typewriter for three hours every day,' I tell him. Besides, I'm the one got him to learn to read and write. Also, I'm the handsomest Indian in at least three provinces . . ."

"This is radio," says Vince. "Girls think I sound handsome. And I never discourage them."

Now Vince is a scrawny little guy with a sunk-in chest and a complexion look like it been done with a waffle iron.

"I just figured me an angle," says Frank.

One thing that puzzles me is how many people actually listen to the radio. I mean *really* listen. We have the radio for background in the truck or on portable radios.

"Sometimes we have over twelve thousand listeners," Vince tell us. "For an area where trees outnumber people a hundred to one, that ain't bad."

We try to behave ourselves when we're at the radio station, and Frank coach Rufus Firstrider, who have a natural talent for electrical things, to see what it is Harvey do to make the station come on the air every afternoon and shut off at night.

One afternoon when I walk down to the station about an hour before opening time, I find Frank Fencepost sitting in the sun reading the Bible.

"Once you learn there's no telling what you'll end up reading," Frank say, smile kind of sickly. We've had lots of people who flog the Bible, from Father Alphonse, who come pretty close to being human, to Pastor Orkin of the Three Seeds of the Spirit, Predestinarian, Bittern Lake Baptist Church, who hate everybody who don't believe just like him.

"You know what I done?" Frank ask.

"Applied to have a sex change?"

Frank stare at me in surprise.

"A lucky guess," I say.

"I got out my Webster's dictionary and I looked up the word gospel. We think of it as all the 'you can't do that or you'll go to hell for sure' stuff. But it really mean 'good news.' I got me some really strong ideas. I just got to figure how I can get Vince to let me talk on the radio."

The day Frank got his Webster's dictionary, about a dozen of us go into the book store in Wetaskiwin. Everybody is looking at something different. I'm actually buying the new book by my favorite author, Tony Hillerman, who write about a kind old

Indian policeman, Lt. Joe Leaphorn, who remind me of Constable Greer, the one really good RCMP in our area. Frank stuff a big dictionary with a rainbow-colored cover under the raincoat he borrowed from Mad Etta without asking and boogie right out of the store.

"I'm the one who needs a good dictionary," I say to Frank in the parking lot.

"Steal your own," says Frank. But later on he get soft-hearted, like Frank usually do, and let me keep the dictionary near to my typewriter, though Frank spend a lot of time at my place reading in it. Frank try to learn a new word every day, and use it in a sentence, which get pretty tiresome when he try to use words like *gleet*, which mean sheep snot, or *sutler*, which mean a person who follows an army and sells them provisions. Not words for everyday conversation.

Every night at suppertime, Rufus Firstrider make a run into Wetaskiwin and come back with lots of fast food. Those forays sure cut into our spending money, but we're willing to help Frank as much as we can. Harvey, when he's full of fatty foods, take Rufus under his wing, and in a week Rufus knows how to turn on the radio station and get Frank's voice out on the airwaves.

We watch the station close up at 11:00 p.m., wait an hour, then Frank open the door like he never heard of the word *lock*.

Before we turn on the lights we hang a heavy blanket over the window.

Rufus fuss with some switches. Then, from his glassed-in cage he signal Frank that it is okay to talk. A big red light come on over the door, say "In Use."

"K-UGH is going to present a special program one hour from now," Frank say. "'Brother Frank's Gospel Hour' will ask the question, 'What does it take to make you happy?' Be sure and tune in."

He make announcements like that every five minutes from midnight to 1:00 a.m. Then at one o'clock he cue up some music that he had me hunt up. The station have only about a hundred tapes. This one's some outfit with bagpipes playing "Amazing Grace."

"Welcome to 'Brother Frank's Gospel Hour.' Brother Frank wants everyone to feel as good as he feels, to be as happy as he is . . ."

And he's off and running.

"Silas," Frank has been telling me for weeks, "I'm gonna combine theology, mythology, history, ritual, and dream. Seems to me that covers everything. Got to have some Christian connection in order to get money, people will give to anything that they even suspect of being religious. And dreams is how we work in the Indian part."

Frank talk for a while about how everybody deserve to feel good, to be happy, to have enough to eat, a dry place to sleep, good friends, and happy dreams.

"Now, what I'm wondering, as I talk to this big, old microphone, is, is there anybody out there? If you're listening, call Brother Frank on the phone," and he give the area code 403, and K-UGH's telephone number. "We accept collect calls. Just let us know you're listening. Tell us what you need to make you happy. And if you got an idea, tell us how we could improve 'Brother Frank's Gospel Hour.' Remember, gospel means 'good news.' And Brother Frank is gonna make good news happen to you."

Frank sigh, and point to Rufus, who flip a switch and a trio start singing "Let the Sunshine In."

Frank has hardly lit up a cigarette when the phone rings.

"'Brother Frank's Gospel Hour,'" I say, in kind of a whisper. I'm betting it's either Vince or Harvey giving us five minutes to clear out of the station or they'll call the RCMP.

"Collect from Jasper, Alberta," say an operator's voice.

"Go ahead."

"Brother Frank is the biggest idiot I ever heard on the radio," say a man's booming voice. He apply a couple of unpleasant curse words to Frank, and a couple more to me, then he slam the receiver in my ear.

"Wrong number," I say. "They wanted a tow truck."

"Hey, I would of got them a tow truck," say Frank. "There is nothing Brother Frank and the power of prayer can't accomplish."

The record is about over before the phone ring again.

"Hello," say what sound like a young woman's voice.

"Go ahead," I say.

"If I tell you what I need to make me happy, what are you gonna do about it?"

"Maybe I should let you talk to Brother Frank," I say.

I nod to Frank. He nod to Rufus who got more music ready to go.

"What can Brother Frank do for you?" Frank ask.

"You really want to know what will make me happy?" say the girl.

"That is Brother Frank's purpose in life."

"I need a CD player and the latest Tanya Tucker CD."

"Don't we all," says Frank, with his hand over the receiver. "Why would that make you happy?"

"Because my parents belong to a religion that thinks music is sinful. I have to sneak my radio on under my covers after they're asleep."

"A day without music is like a day without sex," say Frank. "Give me your name and address and Brother Frank will mail you enough money to buy a CD player and Tanya Tucker." Frank write for a minute. "You start watching the mail. And when you get your own money, you make a contribution to 'Brother Frank's Gospel Hour,' so we can help somebody else."

The girl bubble with thank yous, and promise to send money when she is able.

"See, that wasn't so hard," says Frank.

"Only trouble is we don't have any money to send her," I point out. "All that's gonna happen is she'll watch an empty mailbox for a month or two."

"Never underestimate Fencepost Power," says Frank.

Frank launch right in. "Our motto is, 'Before my needs, the needs of others,'" Frank say, and he explain the girl who live in a house without music and ask listeners to send in a dollar or ten dollars to make other people happy.

Within an hour we got an old lady who need money to pay her heating bill. Another old lady need money to take her pet cat to the vet. And a woman who sound about thirty call to say her husband drunk up the welfare check and her kids is hungry, what will make her happy is a few groceries.

"Wow," says Frank. "I think we touched a nerve."

We get stupid calls, too. Smart-ass guys, sound like Frank just a few weeks ago, want money for beer, or a date with Madonna, or to touch the jockstrap of Mario Lemieux, the famous French hockey player.

Frank, without using any names, tell the stories of the people in need.

"Brother Frank going to see that those little kids don't go hungry, and that lady don't have to be cold, and that cat gets to the hospital. If I have to steal to do it, I will. But you can help. Send what you can, a dollar, five dollars, ten thousand," and Frank chuckle, "to 'Brother Frank's Gospel Hour,' c/o K-UGH Radio," and he give the station's box number in Wetaskiwin.

Frank stay on the air until 3:00 a.m.

"Brother Frank will visit with you again tomorrow. And may *your* Great Spirit, whatever that may be, never rain on your parade."

Rufus shut off the equipment and give Frank the thumbs-up sign like we seen Harvey give Vince.

"From now on, Silas, you pick up Brother Frank's mail every day. Wouldn't want all this money fall into the wrong hands."

We kept expecting Vince or Harvey to discover what we been doing, but Frank keep up his late-night broadcasting.

I check the mail box every day, but there is nothing addressed to "Brother Frank's Gospel Hour."

People's requests all translate into money. The people who call in come mostly from a long way off. That girl without music live in a place called Blueberry Mountain, hundreds of miles up north.

Frank, doing some creative borrowing at a K-Mart in Edmonton, acquire the CD player, but among us all we couldn't raise the postage to mail it.

Connie stand in line at a post office, ask for seven dollars' worth of stamps, then just pick them up and walk out. The clerk yelling like crazy, but not running after her.

"They wouldn't feel so bad if they knew they were contributing to making someone happy," says Frank, as he stuff the parcel into a slot at the main post office.

One morning me and Frank head off to Calgary in Louis Coyote's pick-up truck. Frank, he want to hear an evangelist on a Calgary radio station. This fellow he got a twang in his voice sound like the real Hank Williams used to.

"Entertainment, and touching the heart is what it's all about," says Frank. "I got to have the qualities of a good country singer, a striptease dancer, and . . ."

"A welder," I say.

"Damn right. A good entertainer melt solder with his bare hands. Look into that, Silas. See if there's a magic trick where I can pretend to melt metal."

We figure the place to listen to a radio in comfort would be at my sister's house up in the hills in northwest Calgary. It's been over a year since we visited.

I have to admit Brother Bob treat my sister pretty good, but he been insulting Frank and me ever since he first met us. He sic the police on us more than once, not that we are totally innocent. We one time wreck Brother Bob's new car, and another time we put live horses in his brand new house. Last time here, Frank did a certain amount of damage to the computer system at the finance company my brother-in-law manage. Brother Bob McVey make it clear we ain't welcome at either his home or his business. But we figure time dim the bad things, and we make sure to arrive in the middle of the afternoon.

Only trouble is, he at home.

"How come you ain't off repossessing trucks from poor Indians?" Frank ask when Brother Bob answer the door.

Brother Bob don't look very good. He is wearing a bathrobe and ain't shaved in, I bet, half a week. I always figure Brother Bob woke up already shaved.

He just wave us into the living room, where my sister Illianna patching some of little Bobby's jeans.

"You sick or something, Brother Bob?" I ask.

Brother Bob just stare at "The Price Is Right" on TV. Illianna answer for him. "Bob's been out of work — almost nine months now. He's feeling kind of depressed."

Illianna explain that the big finance company Brother Bob managed went out of business. They loaned millions of dollars to companies in the oil patch, and since the price of oil been going down forever, those companies couldn't pay their loans. The finance company close up after they used up all the company pension fund trying to stay in business. Brother Bob don't get a dime in layoff pay for all his years with the company, plus he lose all his pension money.

"Why don't you get another job?" Frank ask.

"There aren't any jobs in Bob's field. In case you haven't noticed," Illianna answer, "the economy is really bad."

"Sorry," says Frank. "Being unemployed all my life, it's hard to tell."

"I've been trying to get a job," says Illianna, "but it's years since I worked, and then I was just waiting tables. All I could earn as a waitress wouldn't pay the mortgage. Silas, I don't know what we're gonna do."

"I got maybe sixty dollars," I say.

"And you got my good wishes," says Frank. "But I got a scam going that gonna make us all rich. Six months from now Fencepost will offer you a job. Fencepost might even offer Brother Bob a job." Frank consider that possibility for a moment, then say, "Nah."

After that we are kind of uncomfortable. We wait long

enough to give little Bobby a hug when he get home from school, then we listen to the evangelist in the truck at a truck stop on Deerfoot Trail.

On the fifth day there are two letters addressed to "Brother Frank's Gospel Hour." I rush them back to the pool hall and Frank rip them open. One contain a two-dollar bill, the other a useless one-dollar loonie coin.

We is all pretty disappointed.

Frank is getting five to ten calls every night from people in need. It surprising how small people's wants are. A pair of eye-glasses, a toy, shoes, some dental work so someone can look passable when they go job hunting. Frank has written down everybody's requests along with their names and addresses in a notebook. There is close to forty and it don't look like we going to be able to fill none of them.

"If people could just see me in person," says Frank. "I could convince them to part with their money. We'd pay off the needy people and have a lot left over for us. Guess I'm gonna have to do like these real evangelists and beg hard."

Turn out the problem wasn't Frank, but our usual bad mail service. After about eight days, the mail box start to fill up. There is fourteen letters one day, total eighty dollars in cash and checks. The next day there is twenty-six letters, with over a hundred dollars. The lady from Drumheller get her grocery money. The lady from Obed get to pay her heating bill.

That night Frank thank people for their kindness, he get a tear in his voice as he say there is so much to do and so little time and money.

It take Bedelia and me and even Frank's girl, Connie Bigcharles, to talk him out of imitating that famous evangelist, I think it was Oral Robertson, who claim he going to be called to heaven if he don't get enough money donated from his followers.

"For one thing, we don't think you'd be called to heaven," we tell Frank. "For another, Oral Robertson didn't get all the money he craved, and he didn't die."

"All he got, I think, was a toothbrush named after him," says Connie Bigcharles.

"It would attract attention to me," says Frank. "That's what being a celebrity is all about. I read somewhere that unless you get caught in bed with little boys, all publicity is good publicity."

"Or unless, like that other evangelist, you get caught in the back seat of your car with a working girl."

"What's wrong with that?" says Frank. "I been in more back seats than a McDonald's wrapper."

Frank finally see things our way.

"Was that good, or what?" Frank say, after he is off the air. "I never knew I could get that catch in my voice. I figure I'm worth about a thousand dollars a tear from now on."

What Frank say is true.

In another week the requests are only twenty dollars or so ahead of the income. And the prospects are looking righteous. Unfortunately, whenever something is going good, something go wrong.

I only take the mail addressed to "Brother Frank's Gospel Hour." How am I supposed to know that people are writing to K-UGH to say how much they enjoy Frank's program?

One morning when I go to pick up the mail, Vince been there before me.

Vince and Harvey ain't mad. They just want a cut.

"Word will get back to the higher-ups eventually, but until

then, you got a great scam going. We checked in on your broadcast last night. You, Mr. Frank, have got charisma."

"I hear you can get antibiotics for that," says Frank.

For 10 percent off the top, Vince and Harvey agree to be deaf, dumb, and blind to "Brother Frank's Gospel Hour." There was nearly four hundred dollars in that day's mail.

We have to open up a bank account for "Brother Frank's Gospel Hour" at the Bank of Montreal in Wetaskiwin. Frank and me and Bedelia Coyote are the ones who can write checks. Frank cut Bedelia in because she got the stamina to deal with government.

"There is ways for every dollar we take in to be tax free, and I'm gonna research all those ways," Bedelia say.

Another month and Frank just keep getting better. Soon, there is actually money left over when the requests are filled.

"We put a definite five-hundred-dollar limit on what we pay out," Frank says. "I mean, no sex-change operations that ain't covered by medical insurance. No vans for the handicapped, no matter how worthy the cause. Three hundred dollars for bus tickets so Granny can see the daughter and new grandchild is what we're all about. That draw more tears than a $40,000 van for some guy who can only move two fingers and his pecker."

Things get complicated when the newspapers start coming around, wanting to interview Brother Frank. Soon as the stories run, the bigwigs at K-UGH start asking a lot of questions.

Since I am the worrier, I worry we been doing something illegal, and maybe all of us, or especially Frank, could go to jail.

But the bigwigs at K-UGH find that after only six weeks, "Brother Frank's Gospel Hour" draw more listeners at two in the morning than all their regular shows.

Frank get called in to K-UGH, and me and Bedelia go with

him. There is three guys in suits, one come all the way from Toronto, which, they tell us, is where everything really happen.

"Then how come I never been there?" Frank ask. He live life like he got nothing to lose. And I guess that's true. Until now.

The suit from Toronto chuckle politely, then offer Frank a contract and the 9:00 p.m. to 11:00 p.m. broadcast time.

"We'd like to offer you a five-year contract at $60,000 a year, rising $5,000 each year, so by the end of the contract you'll be making $80,000 a year," the Toronto suit say.

"I bet that's almost as much as the guys on 'Stampede Wrestling' make," says Frank.

At this point Bedelia Coyote break into the conversation. Bedelia has studied accounting by mail, and she has studied business management by mail, as well as how to organize a demonstration and how to get your organization's name in the newspaper without committing an indictable offence.

"Mr. Fencepost will be happy with your salary offer," she say, "but we only want a month-to-month contract."

Bedelia have to pull Frank off into a corner and have a pretty loud whispered conversation to get him to agree to that.

"Plus," Bedelia go on, "'Brother Frank's Gospel Hour' manage all the money that is donated. We pick which people get their requests filled, and Mr. Fencepost hire his own support staff and pay them out of the donated money."

The suits argue for quite a while because they had their eyes on the income donated to "Brother Frank's Gospel Hour."

"We can take our program over to CFCW, the country-music station in Camrose. Bet they'd be happy to have us. Or, we might contact one of the big radio stations in Edmonton," say Bedelia.

The suits give in.

I can't believe how fast things move after that. What Frank talk ain't exactly Christianity, but he mention the Bible often enough that Christians like him. He throw in enough fictional Indian mythology, some of which I make up, to what Frank call "make us politically correct."

"Everybody loves the idea of an Indian these days. So look me up a bannock recipe, and I'll include it on tomorrow night's program," he say to me. "And saskatoon pie. We'll tell them where to pick the best saskatoons. The country will be overrun with berry-pickers."

Frank also talk about fulfilling dreams and positive thinking enough that the people who believe in crystal power and having conversations with rocks and trees like him, too.

By the time Frank get settled in his new time slot, Bedelia is negotiating with the big radio stations in Edmonton and some outfit would do something called "syndicate" the show, putting Frank on over one hundred stations, many of them in the United States, where, Frank say, the real money is.

Frank make Bedelia his business manager and me his personal assistant, and he find jobs for Rufus and Winnie Bear, Robert Coyote and his girl Julie Scar, and about ten other of our friends. My salary in a month is as much as I ever made in a year writing books.

One night I try to phone Illianna, but all I get is a guy with a deep voice tell me my call cannot be completed as dialed. After I pretend I'm Frank and get real pushy with Information, they tell me the number I'm calling been disconnected for non-payment.

The day I cash my first check at the Bank of Montreal, I put a hundred-dollar bill in an envelope and address it to Illianna.

At supper one night a couple of weeks later, Ma say, "Illianna phoned Ben Stonebreaker's store and left a message that she coming for a visit."

"That's wonderful," says my sister, Delores. "I just love Bobby."

Bobby is only a year or so younger than Delores.

"That's what makes me worried," says Ma. "She's bringing Bobby, and What's-his-name, and she ask Mrs. Ben Stonebreaker if maybe the Quails' old cabin is available, 'cause they planning to stay for a while." After the Quails build themselves a new house, their old cabin sit vacant with half the windows knocked out and a few strips of what used to be bright green siding bulging loose under the front window.

Ma, over the years, has mellowed some toward Illianna's husband, Robert McGregor McVey. Now it's What's-his-name. She used to refer to him in Cree as He Who Has No Balls.

A few days later, Illianna and her family turn up on the reserve, and I can't help remembering the first time they visit after they been married. Brother Bob was driving a new car with racing stripes and silver hub caps, and we give him an Indian name, Fire Chief, just like the gasoline down at Crier's Texaco garage, and little Bobby was still a glint in Eathen Firstrider's eye.

Today they is driving what white people call an Indian car. It is a huge Pontiac, about a 1972, painted a pumpkin color, full of dents, sagging and clunking, with about a million miles on it, and a big U-Haul trailer with stuff tied all over the outside of it rattles along behind.

"They repossessed the house and the car and the boat and the snowmobile," Illianna say. Little Bobby start crying when he hear the word *snowmobile*. "Thanks for the money, Silas. I used it to put most of our furniture in storage, though I don't know how I'll pay the storage fees."

Brother Bob is, as they say, only a shadow of his former self. His suits hang on him like they was three sizes too big, and even his snap-brim hat seem to sink down over his ears. He hardly talk, and when he do he just sigh and whisper "yes" or "no."

The day we buy about a hundred yards of extension cord from Robinson's Store in Wetaskiwin ("Charge it to 'Brother Frank's Gospel Hour,'" Frank tell the clerk, and get a smile instead of a who-the-hell-are-you look) and run it across a slough and through a culvert from Blue Quills Hall so Brother Bob can hook up his TV to watch the soap operas and Illianna can plug in her microwave, Brother Bob mumble a couple of thanks yous and grip both my hands the way an old person do.

Brother Bob used to look right through us like we didn't exist. And when he did see us, he make bad jokes about our large families, how run down our cars are, and how clean we ain't.

Within weeks word come down that "Brother Frank's Gospel Hour" going international on 112 radio stations. At the same time Bedelia sell a syndicated newspaper column where I write up some of the letters Frank get, and how he send money to those people for the one thing that will make them happy. I tell five stories in every column. Four serious and one that we find funny, one where Frank usually say no. Like the kid who want karate lessons so he can beat up on his teacher. Or the woman who claim she getting messages from Elvis in her back teeth and wants a radio transmitter so she can share the messages.

The number of radio stations expand almost every day and soon television want to get in on the act. One hour, once a week, where they fly in some of the people we been helping.

"I'm gonna be bigger than Oprah," say Frank, when Bedelia

give him the news. "Let me rephrase that. I'm gonna have more listeners than Oprah."

"You wish," says Bedelia. "We're only starting in twelve stations. Besides, Oprah don't beg for money. But when you let that tear ooze out of your eye and run down your cheek, I can hear pens all over North America scratching signatures on checks."

Soon so much money come rolling in we rent Blue Quills Hall and hire Illianna to sort the cash and checks. When she need an assistant we hire my Ma, Suzie Ermineskin, full-time, and my sister, Delores, part-time.

Frank these days is dressing like Johnny Cash, frilly white shirt, black preacher's coat, western bow tie. He look a lot better than the time he wore a fuzzy green cocktail dress and won the Miss Hobbema Pageant.

The TV people want Frank to do a personal appearance tour.

"Forty cities," Bedelia tell Frank. "Starting in Calgary, working to Minneapolis and on to places I never heard of."

Bedelia arrange to buy a used bus, hire a lady sign painter with long red hair to paint tomahawks, eagles, and dream catchers all over the bus, and "'Brother Frank's Gospel Hour,' A Place Where Dreams Come True," down both sides.

The tour give me an idea. I argue loud and long with Frank, but I don't get anywhere until I take Frank for a walk around the reserve.

"What would make you happy?" I ask. "Pretend you could write a letter to 'Brother Frank's Gospel Hour.' What would you ask for?"

Frank stop and think.

"My biggest surprise is that some of the good things haven't made me as happy as I thought. Like renting that Lincoln Continental, and having more groupies than a rock star. The car is nice, but it's just a car. And it was more fun when girls told me to get lost and I had to impress them."

"I know what would make you happy," I say.

"What's that, Silas?"

"Revenge," I say, "against He Who Has No Balls."

I let that sink in for a minute. I wonder if Frank is gonna buy my idea, and what I'm gonna do to help Illianna and little Bobby if he don't.

There is the beginning of a smile on Frank's face. "There is an old saying in the Fencepost clan," Frank say. "Always kick your enemy when he is down."

"This is your chance to really get back at Brother Bob," I say hopefully.

"By golly, Silas, you're right. I can make him suck up to me. I'll make him wear a sissy uniform like a theater usher, and a visored cap with BRO. FRANK in silver letters across the crown."

He grab my shoulder, turn me around, and our pace pick up as we walk in the dark, spruce-smelling air toward Brother Bob and Illianna's cabin.

About the Author

W. P. KINSELLA is the author of several short story collections, including three reissued by SMU Press: *Red Wolf, Red Wolf* (1990), *Shoeless Joe Jackson Comes to Iowa* (1993), and *Go the Distance: Baseball Stories* (1995), originally published as *The Further Adventures of Slugger McBatt*. He is best known for his award-winning novel *Shoeless Joe*, which became the film *Field of Dreams* in 1989. A native Canadian, Kinsella divides his time between western Canada and California.

Shoeless Joe Jackson Comes to Iowa

"KINSELLA . . . DEFINES A WORLD IN WHICH MAGIC
AND REALITY COMBINE TO MAKE US LAUGH AND THINK ABOUT
THE PERCEPTIONS WE TAKE FOR GRANTED."
New York Times

Set in Iowa, urban Canada, and San Francisco, the stories in W. P. Kinsella's *Shoeless Joe Jackson Comes to Iowa* focus on characters who have vivid imaginations and creative means for coping with life's disappointments.

In "Fiona the First," a hung-over aluminum window salesman is a kind of Ancient Mariner doomed to wander Pony Express depots, railway stations, and airports picking up girls. In the title story that grew into the novel *Shoeless Joe* and later became the acclaimed film *Field of Dreams*, baseball, magic, and the redemptive power of fantasy converge in a midwest cornfield. In "A Picture of the Virgin," a clever prostitute cons a gullible young man in an Edmonton brothel, and in "First Names and Empty Pockets," an Iowa mender of broken dolls drinks with the brash young Janis Joplin in a forlorn San Francisco bar.

"IN THE WONDERFUL TITLE STORY . . . [KINSELLA CREATES]
A HEARTBREAKINGLY PERFECT WORLD: IT'S MAGIC . . .
IN A MERE SIXTEEN PAGES."
Los Angeles Times Book Review

ISBN 0-87074-355-4, cloth • ISBN 0-87074-356-2, paper

Toll-free order number: 1-800-826-8911

ALSO AVAILABLE FROM SMU PRESS

Go the Distance: Baseball Stories

"IF THE BASEBALL HALL OF FAME CAN FIND SPACE FOR PINETAR BATS,
IT SURELY SHOULD CREATE A KINSELLA READING ROOM."
USA Today

As in *Shoeless Joe* and his other baseball fiction, Kinsella uses the sport not as subject but as context in these ten stories, which range from the realistic to the fantastic. "For Kinsella," says the *Miami Herald*, "a baseball stadium is a window on the human heart."

In "Searching for Freddy," a sportswriter pursues an elusive Johnny Appleseed of baseball, a base-stealing phenomenon who disappeared years ago after two seasons with the St. Louis Browns and, now a disabled old man, roams the country transmitting the secrets of his gift to promising young athletes. In "Reports Concerning the Death of the Seattle Albatross Are Somewhat Exaggerated," an extraterrestrial masquerades as the Seattle Mariners mascot with tragicomic results. In "K Mart," three middle-aged baseball buddies play a nostalgic pickup game in the women's wear section of the block-long store that now sits on their boyhood playing field.

Seven other stories—about diehard fans, crusty veterans, would-be diamond heroes, and baseball as a boyhood bond—fill out this collection, originally published as *The Further Adventures of Slugger McBatt.*

"KINSELLA IS A WHIZ AT BRINGING CHARACTERS TO LIFE. . . .
[IN GO THE DISTANCE] HE HITS A HOME RUN."
Publishers Weekly

ISBN 0-87074-387-2, cloth• ISBN 0-87074-388-0, paper

Toll-free order number: 1-800-826-8911